THE MAPLIN BIRD

The Maplin Bird

K . M . PEYTON

Illustrated by Victor G. Ambrus

WITH A NEW INTRODUCTION BY
KAREN M. KLOCKNER

GREGG PRESS
BOSTON

Text copyright © 1965 by K. M. Peyton

Reprinted by arrangement with William Collins Publishers

Introduction copyright © 1980 by Karen M. Klockner

New material designed by Barbara Anderson

Gregg Press Children's Literature Series logo by Trina Schart Hyman

Printed on permanent/durable acid-free paper and bound in the United States of America

Republished in 1980 by Gregg Press, A Division of G.K. Hall & Co., 70 Lincoln St., Boston, Massachusetts 02111

First Printing, January 1980

J

P

Library of Congress Cataloging in Publication Data

Peyton, K   M   , psued.
  The Maplin Bird.

  (Gregg Press children's literature series)
  Reprint of the ed. published by World Pub. Co., Cleveland.
  SUMMARY: An orphaned sister and brother become involved with a wealthy smuggler and his operation on the Essex seacoast in the mid-19th century.
  [1. Smuggling—Fiction. 2. England—Fiction. 3. Orphans—Fiction]
  I. Ambrus, Victor G. II. Title. III. Series.
  PZ7.P4483Map 1979   [Fic]   79-18257
  ISBN 0-8398-2611-7

Introduction

K M. PEYTON has received wide acclaim in both England and the United States. Author of over 20 books, she was given the Guardian Award in 1970 for her Flambards trilogy and won the Carnegie Medal in the same year for *The Edge of the Cloud* (1969; published in the U.S., 1970) — the second book in the trilogy. *The Plan for Birdmarsh* (1965; published in the U.S., 1966) was runner-up for the Carnegie Medal in 1965, and in that year *The Maplin Bird* (1964; published in the U.S., 1965) was chosen as an Honor Book for the New York *Herald Tribune* Children's Book Festival.

Born in Birmingham, England, in 1929, Kathleen Wendy Herald grew up in Surbiton and attended Manchester Art School. She married a fellow art student, Michael Peyton, in 1950, and received her teaching diploma the following year. Trained to teach art, she never considered writing as a profession, although it was her first love. "Writing," she says "has always been my favorite way of enjoying myself."[1]

Her first book was published when she was 15, and at the time she had already written six or seven full-length novels. After marrying, she and her husband collaborated on stories and used the name K. M. Peyton to indicate each of their initials. Since the publication of *Windfall* (1962; published in the U.S. as *Sea Fever*, 1963), Ms. Peyton has authored the books on her own, but still retains the pseudonym. Today she lives "in an old farm cottage in a village forty miles from London, our boat moored in a creek ten minutes walk away, the ponies grazing in a field next door. We draw, write, charter our boat and take photographs for a living — and feel that it is a very good arrangement!"[2]

When working together, the Peytons wrote magazine serials, largely to formula, which were later published as books. After it was no longer necessary to continue the enterprise for financial reasons, Ms. Peyton decided to write something for her own pleasure — a book in which she could "ramble on."[3] The result was *Windfall*, which she considers her " 'first pure book.' "[4] Her publisher at the time, Collins, returned the manuscript saying she ought to shorten it and cut out all the philosophical parts — "which of course were what I thought were all the good bits,"[5] she says. So she sent it to Oxford, who accepted it and who continue to publish her books today.

Windfall is the story of a 16-year-old boy who earns his living on a fishing smack and who must support his mother and brothers and sister after his father is knocked overboard and killed. John Rowe Townsend has said, the "storytelling and command of material . . . are superb."[6] Matt encounters numerous difficulties and has breath-taking adventures at sea. The author contrasts his life with that of Francis Shelley, a boy of the same age from an aristocratic family. *Windfall* invites comparison with *The Maplin Bird,* because of the similar setting and because both books explore social class differences in mid-19th century England. Emily, the protagonist of *The Maplin Bird,* is a more well developed character than Matt, but there is a greater emphasis on action in the first book.

Following *The Maplin Bird,* Ms. Peyton wrote *Thunder in the Sky* (1966; published in the U.S., 1967) — again set in her home sailing grounds — but this time the plot required research that went beyond her native knowledge of sailing and the sea. The story takes place during World War I, and describes the experiences of a boy working on a barge that carries supplies from England to Calais. Ms. Peyton talked with old skippers who had worked on the barges, and she sailed the same route they took to France. She believes firmly that "one's books can only be built on one's own experiences"[7] — a belief borne out by the fact that nearly all of her stories are about the things she knows and loves: horses, boats, planes, and the sea.

While writing the Pennington books [*The Beethoven Medal* (1971; published in the U.S., 1972), *Pennington's Seventeenth Summer* (1970; published in the U.S. as *Pennington's Last Term, 1971*), and *Pennington's Heir* (1973; published in the U.S., 1974)], she learned to play the piano. The trilogy came after the Flambards books, and she was attempting to write something completely different on a subject about which she knew very little. Her hero, Patrick Pennington, was a gifted musician — at odds with his family, school, and society. The author confesses that she eavesdropped on a group of school boys while traveling home on the train each week, and modeled Pennington on one of them. So she learned a great deal about music and contemporary youth before she actually went about writing the books.

Flambards (1967; published in the U.S., 1968), *The Edge of the Cloud,* and *Flambards in Summer* (1969; published in the U.S., 1970) were published in the late '60s and have been acknowledged as some of K. M. Peyton's best work. The trilogy traces the heroine Christina from her arrival as an orphan at her uncle's home, Flambards, through her war-torn marriage and eventual return to the house years later. Christina and Emily of *The Maplin Bird* have been described as the author's "two splendid heroines" who "even in their teens, are women, not girls. The last thing a Peyton heroine would ever be is girlish."[8] The author says of them "I think . . . [they] are more or less the same person, and both rather untypical of the period I set them in."[9] Her characters are often orphans or adolescents who are estranged from their parents, and their situation thus forces them to handle difficult problems on their own. Ms. Peyton confesses that "Christina in *Flambards* is what I would like to be, strong and fearless."[10]

Ms. Peyton further explains the fact that she writes almost exclusively about adolescents by saying, "I don't feel I'm a writer who wants to write adult books and has just missed off; I never have that feeling .... I'm very interested in this age ... where young people change so quickly, and are so difficult to understand, in all ways. I can remember those feelings so clearly. It is a fascinating age, and everything matters so much."[11] She also says, "The adult situation bores me. Characters in my mind die on me after the age of twenty."[12] Like many other authors of books for young people, she writes what she wants to write, and her work has found its place in the children's book market.

Her fascination with the emotional changes of adolescence causes her to link books together, thus enabling her to show the development of characters over time. In her two latest books, *Prove Yourself a Hero* (1977; published in the U.S., 1978) and *A Midsummer Night's Death* (1979), Jonathan Meredith is the central character (he first appeared in *The Team,* 1977). A youth in his late teens, Jonathan is kidnapped and held for a large sum of money, which his parents willingly pay. He fears that they will resent the expense later though, and suffers from nightmares and other psychological aftereffects. The book has a contemporary setting and is not a sea story, but it includes some good sailing scenes; for Jonathan is stowed aboard a racing yacht while the kidnappers await the ransom money. *A Midsummer Night's Death* finds him back at school, where a teacher he highly respects is implicated in a murder. Jonathan is the only one who knows, and he agonizes over what to do with the information. The focus is again on the psychological trauma of the central character.

This focus shows an apparent shift in the author's work over the years. Clearly, the "philosophical bits" of which she was so fond in *Windfall* have gradually taken precedence over the action. It cannot be said that the books now lack excitement or adventure, for both of those elements are still present in abundance. But the balance has shifted — the adventurous has given way to the introspective.

K. M. Peyton's central characters often struggle over ethical decisions, but she "denies a specific moral intention in her books."[13] In fact she claims that she writes first because she loves to and also to entertain. Critics have often said her plots sound trite, and she acknowledges this truth: "If you sum up the plot, it's been done so many times, they're so hackneyed, and they all sound so *unworthy,* if you just put them in a few words. They sound terrible."[14] In contrast, she is continually praised for her method, "the exactness, the psychological accuracy, the grace and humour and cool, flowing ease of it all."[15]

The Maplin Bird reveals the roots of her mature style — the vivid quality of descriptive passages, the gift for telling a good story, the ability to evoke an authentic setting and to develop interesting, well-rounded characters. The book is set during the mid-19th century in a coastal fishing village of England. The *Maplin Bird* is a black sailing yacht which was used for running brandy into England from France. Emily Garland first sees the boat as a wooden model in the room of Adam Seymour, the son of the woman for whom she works. Before she realizes the connection between the boat, the man, and his illegal activities, she has become quite fond of him and they have developed a comraderie formerly lacking in the stiff, formal household. So she protects his secret, and when the boat is eventually captured by the customs officials, Adam asks Emily's brother Toby for help in regaining it. Emily and Toby are orphans, and the money Adam offers Toby as well as the fact that he is a friend of Emily's persuades him to undertake the dangerous venture. The arrangement is made without Emily's knowledge, and when the attempt fails and Toby is brought to the Seymour household to recuperate from his injuries, her opinion of Adam is shaken. Adam continues to try to evade the law, and his next escape effort involves both Toby and Emily.

One notable weakness in the book is its episodic nature, which is most likely a hangover from the author's early journalistic training. A series of adventures is woven together by the motives of the various characters, whose paths continue to cross in unexpected ways. Another shortcoming is that although the development of the central character is exceptional, many of the secondary characters are flat and stereotypical. John Rowe Townsend faults the author for making Adam too much the dashing romantic hero, and Marcus Crouch sees Uncle Gideon as too unremittingly cruel to be believed. Another reviewer forgives such flaws, however, saying "the quality of the writing . . . . lifts it head and shoulders above the majority of similar sea-smuggling stories."[16]

The quality of the writing may be likened to a tightly woven fabric — sometimes with the texture of a knobby wool, at other times like fine linen. Heavily laden with the technical language of sailing, which may be unfamiliar to some readers, the prose nevertheless conveys a strong feeling for the sea and for boats: "With an inch of the tiller one way and then the other, an eye on his swollen staysail, he threaded *My Alice* through her sisters, shaving bowsprits and stern with what seemed to Emily incredible luck. Or was it judgment?" (p. 32). K. M. Peyton balances the joyous exhilaration of running under full sail with the miserable experience of seasickness, the struggle of sailing at night through a storm, and the cold, cramped quarters of the cuddy below board.

The character of Emily has been described as "resourceful, spirited, [and] enduring" by John Rowe Townsend, who says that she "steals the story entirely from her brother Toby."[17] If it is true that the other characters serve largely as foils for Emily's development, the author's method is not ineffective. Emily is a heroine of calm, sustaining courage and the author balances the adventurous side of her story with Emily's thoughtful, sensitive nature. She created Emily out of her own experience and says, "Everything Emily suffered in the smack 'My Alice' in *The Maplin Bird* I had suffered,"[18] and "what was happening to me in my sailing life was more shattering than anything endured by Emily on board her smack; writing of her sufferings came very easily after my own shipwreck and rescue."[19] Here again, it is when writing of the things she knows intimately that the author is at her best.

She has been criticized both by herself and by others for having a strong romantic streak. In *The Maplin Bird,* the romance may be seen in Toby and Emily's escape from Uncle Gideon, in the character of Adam Seymour, and in the adventures which occur at sea. Emily struggles with her romantic dreams and yearnings, constantly chastising herself for not being satisfied with what life has given her. She sees Adam for the hard-hearted smuggler he is but cannot deny a fascination with him. For Emily, as well as for Adam and his sister Selina, the constrictions of everyday life are a torment. Emily likens her role as a maid in the Seymour household to the prospect of imprisonment for Adam. She reflects that

> all her life till now, she had been free to wander along the sea walls and the strips of shingle; it had been as natural to her as breathing, the sky and the smell of the Essex mud. The smell of dust and polish choked her when outside the windows the sun was shimmering across the wet mud flats. (p. 97)

Many of K. M. Peyton's characters feel a closeness to nature and are happiest when running along a beach, galloping on a horse, or holding the tiller of a boat. The integration of action and introspection occurs in the earlier as well as in the later books. But the romanticism is not an untempered one; the glorious moments of joy occur only with the knowledge that they cannot last.

The theme of freedom from societal constrictions is linked to the author's portrayal of class differences in *The Maplin Bird*. The life of Emily and Toby is contrasted with that of the affluent Seymour household. Emily and Toby are bound to a grueling schedule of work in order to survive, while Adam and Selina Seymour are frustrated and bored by their aimless existence — the life of the very rich. Adam begins smuggling for the sheer excitement of it, and Selina pleads with her mother for permission to go to college — considered an unladylike pursuit at the time. Emily is aware of the ironic contrast in lifestyles but is surprised to learn that Selina envies and admires her. Similarly, in *Windfall,* Francis Shelley longs to know the experience of fishing every day on the smacks. And in *A Pattern of Roses* (1972; published in the U.S., 1973), Peyton parallels the comfortable life of Tim in mid-20th century England with that of Tom, a working-class boy living in the Edwardian age. Tim eventually chooses to forego his expensive education in favor of apprenticing himself to a blacksmith. Here and elsewhere, Ms. Peyton values the "perfect spiritual grace" which Tim strives for and which Tom has unknowingly achieved.

In *The Maplin Bird* and other earlier books these themes are first introduced. In later works the same ideas and characters emerge more fully. They are evidence of an integrity on the part of the author which has grown and matured and constantly found newer forms of expression. Each book reflects a different side of the author's personality, for she has never been satisfied to slide backwards on her fame. *The Maplin Bird* is a book which stands on its own but which also forms a step in the evolution of an outstanding talent.

Karen M. Klockner
Boston, Massachusetts

References

1. *The Third Book of Junior Authors,* ed. by Doris D. Montreville and Donna Hill (Bronx, New York: H.W. Wilson Company, 1972), p. 225.
2. *The Third Book of Junior Authors,* p. 225.
3. Justin Wintle and Emma Fisher, *The Pied Pipers: Interviews with the Influential Creators of Children's Literature* (New York: Paddington Press, Ltd., 1974), p. 264.
4. *Twentieth Century Children's Writers,* ed. by D.L. Kirkpatrick (New York: St. Martin's Press, 1978), p. 996.
5. *The Pied Pipers,* p. 264.
6. John Rowe Townsend, *A Sense of Story: Essays on Contemporary Writers for Children* (Boston: The Horn Book, Inc., 1971), p. 173.
7. *The Thorny Paradise: Writers on Writing for Children,* ed. by Edward Blishen (Great Britain: Kestrel/Penguin Books, 1975), p. 124.
8. *A Sense of Story,* p. 178.
9. *A Sense of Story,* p. 179.
10. *The Pied Pipers,* p. 266.
11. *The Pied Pipers,* p. 265.
12. *The Thorny Paradise,* pp. 123–4
13. *The Pied Pipers,* p. 263.
14. *The Pied Pipers,* p. 266.
15. Louis Claibourne, *The Spectator* (November 13, 1971) in *Children's Literature Review,* Volume III (Detroit: Gale Research Company, 1978), p. 172.
16. *The Junior Bookshelf* (November, 1964) in *Children's Literature Review,* Vol. III., p. 177.
17. *A Sense of Story,* p. 174.
18. *A Sense of Story,* p. 179.
19. *The Thorny Paradise,* p. 123.

Contents

Toby's Decision

"And that's for your laziness, young Tobias! And that's for your clumsiness! Get out of my sight before I break your head open, good-for-nothing!"

Young Tobias's sister Emily, scouring an iron pan in the sink in the scullery, shut her eyes and flinched as if she could take the blows for her brother. She heard Toby's footsteps stumble across the flags, and the stubborn thump of his boots on the stairs, not hurrying, not lagging, but stubbornly purposeful as he went to take refuge upstairs. No other sound came from him and Emily knew it would not. Toby did not intend to gratify his uncle that way.

"And where's our supper, you pack of women?" the angry voice bawled again through the scullery door. Emily dropped the pan as her Aunt Mary thrust a cloth and a ladle at her.

"For mercy's sake, don't keep them waiting. I'll bring the plates. The temper he's in!"

Emily hurried out of the scullery and into the kitchen where the three men, her uncle Gideon Boot and his two sons, Charlie and Mark, were sitting down at the scrubbed table. As she fumbled the heavy stew pot off the fire and onto the side of the range to dish up, she heard her uncle raise his voice behind her. What he said was for her benefit, although he spoke to his sons.

"The lad doesn't earn his keep. He's more trouble than he's worth. God knows what Joseph Garland taught him the past three years on that old smack of his."

"Aye, but Uncle Joseph made enough money when he was alive," Charlie said, "and he had no one but Toby to help him."

He did not dare say more in support of his young cousin. He had already said more than enough. Mark growled, "Why do you stick up for him? Father only took him for charity. You know it. And the girl."

Emily could feel his eyes on her back, taunting her. Mark was cruel deliberately. It was worse than his father's cruelty, which was merely the erupting of his uncontrollable temper. The last was bad enough, but. . . . If Mark could feel the bitterness in Emily's eyes as she lugged the stew across to the table he made no sign. Emily had a wild longing to up-end the boiling pot on his thick greasy head. If he thought jibes about charity could hurt her, he could think again. Nobody who worked as hard as she did in this humorless household had any reason to think he did not earn his keep. Perhaps he sensed the red temper in her, for he turned his head and grinned maliciously.

"God knows where she got her temper from. Not from her parents. They were too gentle to live. And they didn't," he added, as if in satisfaction at the innate justice of their fate.

Emily threw the ladle into the stew pot and went back into the scullery. She did not dare say anything. A year ago she would have wept angrily and uselessly in her cloister, the scullery, but eighteen months of Mark's jibes and his father's violence had hardened her. At least she had learned to stop the hurt showing, which she hoped was the same thing. Mark could scarcely get any satisfaction from a clattering ladle.

"Oh, the brutes!" she said softly.

Through the broken pane in the kitchen window the evening smell of the ebbing tide came in, pungent and salt-fresh over the heavy smell of cooking. It smelled of far better things than occupied her mind just then. Emily opened the back door to smell it and think hard about the good things in order to stop herself thinking about what Mark had said. There was nothing wrong with the view, between the outhouses, of the tawny marsh grass, laid over softly by the spring westerlies that were blowing, and the silver line of the estuary above the sea wall. On the far side, two miles away, a few lights shone on Mersea Island, and above them two early stars shone. The sky was violet with dusk. It was March, and warm. She could see the smacks' topmasts in what the village was pleased to call its harbor: the shallow breast of water sheltered from the sea by a strip of marsh grass known as Pewit Island. Somewhere along the saltings, stranded in the mud, lay the smack her father had worked when he was alive, but she couldn't see its mast from the kitchen. Toby had been happy then, working on *My Alice*. She had been happy too, had she but known it, in the Garland cottage three down from Uncle Gideon's. A smacksman called Williams lived in it now, and Emily did not turn her glance that way, for she knew that the sight of the white rose that her mother had planted, waving over the roof of the scullery, had more power to hurt than anything else that was left.

"Get Toby down. He can eat his meal out here," Aunt Mary said in her scolding, harassed voice. "We can't starve the lad. And take your uncle a knife."

Emily took a knife out of the drawer and into the kitchen, and then went upstairs to Toby. The stairs led straight out of the kitchen and were black and steep. At the top, three doors opened left, right, and straight ahead. She knew that Toby would be in the small room, which was her own. Although he slept with his cousins, Toby considered Emily's little room his refuge. She went in. Toby was standing at the window, staring out over the estuary, his hands plunged into his trouser pockets and his shoulders hunched. He glanced at Emily when she came in, and she saw the red marks of Uncle Gideon's fist at the side of his mouth, and a fleck of blood on his lip.

"Maryboot says you can eat in the scullery. She's put it out for you."

Maryboot and Giddyboot was what they had privately called their aunt and uncle when they were small and sometimes now the use of the old nicknames was a comfort, suggesting an independence which, although far from real, was pleasant to pretend. But Toby did not reply.

"Come on," said Emily. "You must be hungry."

Toby, at sixteen a year older than herself, was by nature as resilient as a willow twig and careless as a wind-blown leaf. Laziness and clumsiness, the two vices he had been beaten for, were not in his character, Emily knew—but a magnificent scorn of his uncle and cousins was. Although he was much quieter than he was in the old days, he did not often brood over his ill treatment, if only to show his uncle that he didn't care. But now there was a seriousness in his face Emily hadn't seen before.

"What's the matter? Did he hurt you?"

Toby shook his head. "Listen, Emmy—" He glanced at the open door. "I want to talk to you," he said softly, "but not here. We'll have to go out."

"All right. After supper. We can go for a walk along the sea wall. It's a lovely evening."

Toby nodded.

"Come down now then. I'll hurry with the dishes."

They ate in the scullery and Emily hurried with her jobs, wondering what was on Toby's mind. Usually after supper, if he wasn't tired, Toby went along to spend an hour or two with one of his friends, where he enjoyed the only bit of congenial company left to him; after twelve hours work-

ing on Gideon Boot's smack, day in, day out, it was his only relaxation. Tonight he ate in silence and waited impatiently while she cleared away and fetched her old woolen shawl. Their uncle shouted after them as they went out, but a sense of urgency sent them scurrying away out of reach across the backyard and into the fields.

"He's had sixteen hours' work out of me today," Toby said, "and a round twelve out of you, and none of it costs him a penny, so he's no reason to complain."

"We get our keep," Emily pointed out, to be fair.

"Precious little else," Toby said firmly. "Apart from beltings."

The grass was wet and cold and Emily pulled up her skirt to keep it from getting wet. The hem was worn and beginning to tear and she only had her Sunday one besides, and didn't see where another one was going to come from. They crossed the rough grass to the sea wall and climbed up. A narrow, gravelly beach below them gave directly on to the water, and Emily stopped and lifted her head. After the dingy kitchen and the cooking and the chores and the bickering, the wide, cold ebb, flickered over with the reflections of the first stars, was freedom itself. The sea and the river joined here; to the east the sea wall curved away and the coast shrank back from the blunt embrace of the North Sea. Emily looked out beyond it and saw the tiny moving starboard light of a sail making out from the Colne on the tide, heading south. It might have been going to paradise, the way she felt that moment. The wind was warm and it pulled at the heavy bundle of her hair and loosened long strands that flicked across her face. She jumped down on the wet shingle and ran down the beach until she was breathless, until the North Sea air, cold and salty, was stinging her lungs and her shoes were full of gravelly shells.

"Hey, crazy!" Toby shouted after her from the sea wall. "What do you think you are? A pony?"

"Yes, why not? It's the same as being let loose. That's what I feel like," Emily said, sitting on the sea wall to empty her shoes. Toby stood on the path above her, looking down at her impatiently. Emily remembered that the wind and the smell of the water was as familiar to him as the steamy atmosphere of the kitchen at home was to her; it was his natural setting, and he was hardly likely to share her nonsense. She calmed down, remembering his seriousness. But the air smelled of summer already, in March. She could not ignore it.

"I'm sorry," she said. "What was it you wanted to talk about?"

She glanced at him as he came down and sat on the sloping stones of the sea wall beside her. She could see the swelling on his lip, and the shadow of an old bruise at the corner of his eye.

"Listen, Emmy," he said. "I've decided to go away."

She was instantly startled out of her frivolous mood. It was as if the cold tide came up with his words and ran through her bloodstream. She stared at him.

"Where will you go? You can't! There's no one else—"

"Emmy, I can't go on with them! You must see that. What future is there for me?" The words burst out of Toby as if he had had them bottled inside him for weeks. "I work my guts out for them, day in, day out, and I don't get so much as pocket money! I thought if I waited a while, they'd agree to my taking my father's smack in a year or so and working on my own, but now it seems they've decided to refit *My Alice* and Mark is to have her, with me as his hand! They were talking it over today."

"But they can't do that," Emily said. "*My Alice* is ours. She's ours by law. She's the only thing of any value father left."

"Yes, try telling that to Uncle Gideon! I did and he nearly knocked my head off for my pains. He said his giving us a roof over our heads and enough food to eat made us his wards, and our possessions his. It's rubbish of course, but it seems he's made up his mind. He's already bought new rigging for her, so he's in earnest. But once Mark's got his hands on her, and she's sailing again with all their new gear aboard, what chance shall I have to get her back? To say she's ours? It will be too late then."

"You want to go away with the smack then? Is that what you mean?"

"Yes."

"Where will you take her?"

"I thought to Southend. Father had a friend there—do you remember we went to visit him once? The only time we ever went to Southend. He went shrimping in a bawley. He might help me until I get started, lend me a shilling or two until I get my first catch. But then I'll be working to some purpose, Emmy. I'm no more than a slave at the moment."

"But, Toby—" Emily's world was shattered. She couldn't imagine life at Uncle Gideon's without Toby. Toby was impetuous and wild; he had never been an earnest, responsible boy. Did he really mean what he was saying? She looked at him closely in the dusk. He was staring out at the water, and he looked as determined—even desperate—as she had ever seen him. His chin was lifted; the wind ruffled the thick red-brown hair that fell in an untidy curling mat down the back of his neck. The familiarity of the profile released a rush of awful sentiment in Emily's mind. He was her only link with the old happiness, and the thought of his leaving her alone at Uncle Gideon's was unbearable. She remembered how, when her mother had realized that the cholera was taking her the same way as her husband, she had said to her, "Look after Toby." Not to Toby, "Look after Emily," although Toby was the elder. Emily had often wondered about it, and the words came back to her now. She realized suddenly that her fears now were for Toby, setting out to make his own way in the old smack, *My Alice,* rather than for herself left behind. She felt that she was the stronger, and that her mother had known it.

There was a short silence, then Emily said, "How will you do it? You'll never get away without their catching you."

The determination gave way to a boyish excitement, as Emily had known it would.

"Oh, yes, I will," he said. "If I time it right."

"She'll need a springtide to float her off the mud."

"Yes, of course. She only floats at springs now. A high springtide about midnight, when the wind's blowing westerly, that's what I want." He paused. "March the twenty-first," he added. "If the wind serves."

"You've got it worked out already!" Emily said sharply.

"Well, it *needs* a lot of working out," Toby said, slightly on the defensive. "I don't want to get caught, do I? I can't afford to make mistakes. Uncle Gideon would just about kill me if he caught me red-handed."

"You really mean to go? You've been thinking about it before, not just suddenly?"

"No. I've always thought about it. But now I must go, before Mark gets his hands on the smack."

He turned eagerly to Emily. "Look, Emmy, if I make my way all right you can join me and we'll get a cottage of our own, away from those slave drivers back there." He jerked his head back in the direction of the village. "I can make a living with the smack. We shan't starve."

Emily looked at him, half in doubt, half in excitement. A cottage of their own, independence, had been her pipe dream for months, but she could not believe it would ever be more than a dream. A living was not easy to come by. "It's a pity you're a girl, else you could work the smack with me."

"I can get work. Southend is a busy place since the railway came, they say. There are a whole lot of houses going up, and hotels for the sea bathing. There must be more jobs than there are here, at least."

The light of excitement had come into Emily's eyes. She saw herself in the hallway of a glittering hotel, taking the coats of elegant gentlemen, and perhaps a shilling pressed into her hand, and afterward dining in the kitchen off the roast lamb and chicken sent down from the dining room. Somewhere in his vision there was also the cottage, snug on the sea front, with a fire in the grate where Toby would warm himself when he came in from the smack. This fleeting picture was quenched almost as soon as it came by Emily's staunch common sense.

"I dare say we wouldn't starve," she permitted herself. But she was torn between excitement and an instinctive fear of the unknown. She had scarcely left the village in her life, save for an occasional outing in a farm cart to Burnham or up the river in *My Alice* to Maldon and, once, to Colchester. Toby saw the gleam, and the doubt.

"You don't want to be a slave all your life, do you?" he said. "A skivvy, that's what you are, the same as me."

"There's worse," said Emily briefly.

"There's better too."

"I'm not arguing. It's just that the idea of going away is a shock. Now, at least, we have a roof over our heads, and plenty to eat. It's a big thing, to go away."

"We can live on *My Alice* and eat shrimps," Toby retorted. "And not get beaten for it. Anyway, I'm going."

He got up, and threw a stone into the black water. Emily watched him angrily. She knew that she was going too, as surely as the pebble had dropped into the water.

Toby was wiry and hard. The shabby old clothes of his father's that he wore did not conceal a lively, animal grace in his way of moving. His cousins, Charlie and Mark, were heavily built and heavy of feature, but Toby, like Emily, had inherited something of his mother's firm beauty. It showed in the liveliness of his brown eyes and the eloquence of his dark eyebrows. Emily loved him passionately, for he was all she had, but she found it hard to picture him, scruffy and devil may care, diligently earning them a living amongst the fishermen on the Thames. She prepared for his flight with a stubborn hopefulness that could hardly be called optimism.

For herself she had even less hope, and she kept putting off in her mind any firm decision as to what she would do. In her heart she knew she would have to go with him, but she had no trade like Toby and without anyone to speak for her, with no references and not even a respectable dress, she did not see that anyone in a strange town would be likely to employ her. She had never been to school, for when she was small, in the late eighteen fifties, there was no compulsory education and all she had learned—she could read and write—she had learned from her mother. She could sew and clean and cook after a fashion, but so could the meanest girl. Before her parents fell ill it had been arranged that she should go to work as a dairymaid on a local farm; but her father had gotten her the promise because one of the smacksmen was the farmer's brother, and the promise had been a favor. But after her parents had died in the epidemic, Aunt Mary had taken her into her own home to help her, and would not hear of her going to the farm. For the boys in the village there was no problem. They worked on the smacks with their fathers, or on the farms. Toby had started on *My Alice* the summer he was eight, and was working full time two years later.

Emily knew that she and Toby had a lot to thank their

parents for—she knew it now more than ever. They had been hard working, intelligent, and scrupulously honest. They had rarely argued, nor had her father spent all he earned at the "Green Man." Joseph Garland had been a quiet man, kind and good-humored, and his wife, he had always maintained—correctly—was "a good cut above the rest of the village lasses." She had had both brain and beauty, and Emily remembered her as infinitely just, and patient, and cheerful. Sometimes, during her work amongst the Boot family, Emily wondered if her parents had not grown by comparison more kind and more good-natured and more estimable in every way in her memory than they had in fact been. The old life was like paradise in her mind. But if they had, the memory was the only good thing she had in her life, and she cherished it. The agony of their loss was over. Emily had the sense to hold onto what could do her any good, and forget the rest.

The two weeks before Toby's planned departure seemed to her more ravaged by quarrels and domestic misery than ever. Because time was suddenly limited, it seemed that everything that occurred had a more than usual significance. Gideon Boot was more drunk and more brutal, Aunt Mary— herself goaded by her husband's temper—shrewish and bitter. Outside, the air was warm. Skylarks were shrilling up from the sea wall into a sky glazed with cloud as thin as gauze. If Emily had had any doubts, the shrilling of the skylarks decided her. It was no time for being cautious, choosing a miserable security when they had a boat to sail away in like children in a fairy tale. With the smell of summer the escapade was suddenly gilded with promise of fortune. Emily forgot about her ragged clothes and the prospect of the workhouse and her eyes shone as she

scrubbed the flags under her cousins' muddy boots. Toby
was quiet and anxious. In the evenings he went down to the
saltings to see how *My Alice* lay, to eye his course out of
the shallow creek and into the safety of deep water. The
technical difficulties of getting *My Alice* sailing efficiently
after her eighteen-month sojourn in the Blackwater mud
occupied his mind completely. There would be no time to
prepare anything, only to go aboard, bend on the sails which
were stowed below, and get her moving. The fact that her
rigging was neglected and some of her caulking loose did
not comfort him. But he could repair nothing beforehand,
in case the work was noticed. The tides were making
steadily, each high tide coming up a few inches deeper
over the saltings. *My Alice* lay well back against the sea
wall, and the tide lapped around her weathered hull, but
she did not lift. On the night of the full moon she would
lift, Toby told Emily; then the tides would fall off and she
would be left like a stranded whale once more, and their
chance would be gone. Every night Emily watched the
moon. Sometimes it hid in bright clouds, then it would
sail out over the estuary, brilliant but thin on one side, four
or five days short of its full glory. Emily hated its proud
certainty. Mistress of the tide, the moon would pull it to its
fullest extent on the twenty-first of March, and after that,
if Toby were ready or not, she would let it fall away. The
moon cared nothing for their plots. She was as cold and inexorable as Gideon Boot himself.

On the nineteenth of March Toby came home with a
bloody swelling over one eye that made Emily draw in her
breath. It was his reward, she gathered, for letting the deck
mop go overboard. While he sat eating his supper, his uncle
and Mark and Charlie pulled their chairs up around the

fire—Toby had had to wait till they had finished—and
Mark said suddenly, "It's the height of springs in two days,
Father. How about getting the old smack out? We could
have her sailing in a month, I reckon."

"*My Alice?* Aye. We'll do it. Strip her rigging and get
new on. The sails are good."

Emily, wiping the table, looked at Toby and saw him
hesitate. His eyes gleamed for a moment. Then he went
on eating, and said nothing. Mark turned round and laughed
coarsely.

"And if you lose deck mops when I'm your skipper, I'll
close both your eyes for you."

"Lot o' use he'd be to you then," Charlie said quietly.

"That's the only way scum'll learn," Mark said. "S'like
training a dog."

He tipped his chair back comfortably, and drank his tea
with noisy sips. His father grinned. Toby went on eating,
apparently indifferent, but Emily noticed how his fingers
gripped his fork, as if he would break it in two.

When the men had all gone down to the "Green Man"
and Aunt Mary was dozing by the fire with her mouth
open, Emily put down the sewing she had been left with
and went to Toby who was running the cold pump water
over his eye out in the yard.

"What shall we do?" she said.

Toby straightened up, brushing the water off his face
with his sleeve.

"I'm going tonight," he said.

"But will she lift tonight? It's two days short," Emily
breathed, in anguish.

"If she won't lift," Toby said fiercely, "I'll *carry* her."

The Spring Tide

Emily felt as panic-stricken as if the idea of going had never entered her head before.

"Am—am I coming too?"

"If you want," Toby said, as if he didn't care.

Emily sought around in her head for some reason why they should put off the flight.

"If you wait a little," she said, "they'll have moved the smack for you. It would be easier."

"Aye, and stripped her rigging too. A long way we'll get in that state!" Toby said scornfully.

"But if we wait till there's new rigging on, it will be to our advantage."

"What, and if we're caught be accused of stealing? No. As she is, *My Alice* is ours, every sheet and shackle of her, but once Mark starts work on her, even if he leave his tools aboard and we take them, they can say we are thieves." Toby shook his dripping hair back impatiently. "I've thought about it long enough, Emmy. I've thought of all this long ago. You can see I'm right, surely?"

She nodded slowly.

"What time is the tide tonight then?"

"Twelve. A bit early to suit us, but it could be worse.

They're generally in bed and snoring by ten. We'll get the sails on her when we're in deep water. We'll pole her out, you see—if she lifts. There are sweeps on board. And the wind serves us, look—a westerly, and light. The ebb'll take us away if the wind fails us. It could be a lot worse, Emmy."

As he spoke the hardness went out of his voice and he became enthusiastic, like the old Toby. Emily's panic subsided, and gave way to agonizing doubt.

"Do you think I should come now, or join you later?" Even as she spoke she knew she could not let him go on this adventure alone. Before he could reply, she added, "Oh, let me come! I cannot bear to stay with them. And besides, I shall be useful. I know my way about a smack. How shall we get out of the house without them hearing? The stairs creak dreadfully."

"They all sleep like the dead," Toby said. "And snore besides. Even Aunt Mary. Anyway, we needn't use the stairs. We'll go out through your bedroom window and down the scullery roof. It's simple."

The moon was coming up, with one side still slightly faded. The slates on the scullery roof gleamed invitingly.

"Yes, that part should be easy enough," Emily said.

"If the smack lifts, that's the big question."

That, the crux of the plan, was beyond their power to decide. But Emily, now action was promised, found her mind roving on practical problems.

"We ought to take some food, and water. I'll fetch something out of the pantry while Aunt Mary's asleep, and hide it out here in the yard so that we can pick it up as we go."

There was fresh bread in a crock in the pantry, and half a pie in a basin. Emily knew it was unlikely that anyone would go to the pantry before morning, so she helped herself and carried her haul out into the yard. Wrapped in her apron, they hid it behind the wood pile.

"Let's hope the mice don't get it before we do," Emily said.

A wine-making jar was rescued from a festoon of cobwebs in the back porch, cleaned under the pump, filled with fresh water, and lodged away with the food. It seemed a good omen to them that now, when their plans had to be carried out without warning, they had the opportunity, with the men away and Aunt Mary dozing, to make their preparations. The night was fine and the wind fair. Emily felt her excitement rising, and her fears giving way to a trembling, tingling optimism. She went indoors and tiptoed upstairs. In her cramped bedroom lay all her possessions—and they took up no more room than the small trunk they were packed in. Besides what she was wearing, she owned two darned petticoats, two nightdresses, two blouses, three aprons, a gray woolen skirt, a woolen jacket, a muslin dress, a shawl, a hat, a prayer book, a picture of some geese flying over the marshes, her mother's wedding ring, a china dog, a brush and comb, and a photograph of her mother and father, looking nervous and unfamiliar, in a wooden frame. She spread the shawl out on the bed, and the other clothes and objects she piled on it.

"A fine rich heiress you are, Emily Garland," she said to herself, surveying the unimpressive heap.

Her aunt had gone through the Garland house the day after her sister had died, packing away in her own linen chest every article of clothing and household linen, and stocking her kitchen with the pans, china, and utensils. The furniture had been carted away and sold and the ornaments and oddments thrown away or given away. The picture, the photograph, and the dog Emily had rescued herself from the junk heap; the wedding ring and the prayer book were the only things Aunt Mary had actually given her to keep.

"What if you'd still got the kitchen dresser and the big clock?" she said to herself. "You'd scarcely be going down the scullery roof with *them* tonight."

The thought almost made her giggle. She went to the window and looked out. It was almost dark, but the moon promised to hide very little of their adventure; already the outhouse cast a heavy shadow across the brick paving, and the tiles of the scullery roof were lit like a stage. Emily felt stifling hot and unbearably restless. Looking out of the window and across the estuary, she could picture in infinite

detail the way they would ease *My Alice* out of her berth and get her sailing; beyond that, she had neither the wish nor the imagination to picture anything at all.

She leaned out of the window, staring down at the untidy yards along the row. The place was home, even if she had no feelings for the people. The thought struck her suddenly and extinguished a little of the excitement. She had been born in the house next door but one, and so had Toby. She belonged to this unpicturesque tumble of outhouses and salty grass and tidal mud. The curlews and the skylarks were a part of her. Southend owed her nothing, but Bradwell was in her bones.

"And a fine future you've offered us," Emily said darkly, to Bradwell, to quell the useless affection that rose up just when it was least welcome. "We don't want you."

She went downstairs and finished her sewing; then, when she heard the boots of her uncle and cousins coming up the flag stones, she escaped to her room. It was nine o'clock. Generally the family was in bed and asleep by ten. Toby was in bed but not, Emily supposed, asleep. For herself, she could not even make the pretense of getting into bed.

She took the pins out of her hair and shook it loose down her back and brushed it out. It came down to her hips, springy flying hair which she found difficult to keep tidy, a tawny brown in color and with the shine on it of common health. Emily was wiry like Toby; "slender" she called herself, but Toby called her skinny. (She always reckoned she could get her waist down to the fashionable eighteen inches with the help of a little whalebone, but there was no incentive in the down-to-earth fishing village to be fashionable to that extent.) Her collarbones stuck out but her arms were round enough. Her hands, coarsened by work, were fine-boned but strong, her face alert, dominated by rather fierce blue eyes. Her skin was clear and pale and slightly freckled over the nose. In the summer it went slightly gold, not red, or brown like a gypsy. If she had any vanity, it was her skin that pleased her. She plaited her hair, bundled all her belongings together in her dirty apron, put the shawl around her, and waited. She heard Charlie come up to bed in the same room as Toby, then Mark. Then, at half-past nine Uncle Gideon came up, and last Aunt Mary. She waited another hour, by which time she was so full of fears and borebodings that she would gladly have unbundled her belongings and gotten into bed to forget the whole project. But then she heard the latch click on her door and Toby was there. She leaped to her feet.

"What's all that?" he hissed as she picked up her bundle.

"My things, of course!" she hissed back.

He made an impatient gesture but she took no notice. The window was off the latch. She pushed it open and they looked out.

"You go first," Toby said. "Take off your shoes. I'll bring all this rubbish. Anyone'd think you were emigrating!"

Emily pulled up her skirts and wriggled out through the window. Her clothes made what was really a simple maneuver awkward and dangerous, but she gained the gutter below without accident, and Toby slid her bundle and the shoes carefully down to her. She caught them and dropped them into the yard below. Toby climbed out of the window and shut it behind him, and slid down to join her. A loose slate came with him, but he caught it deftly before it dropped, and lodged it in the gutter which was barely six feet from the ground. They jumped down, put on their shoes and, pausing only to collect the food and water, hurried out of the backyard.

"She's moving!"

"She's not," said Toby dourly.

"I thought I felt her rock." Emily jumped on *My Alice's* deck but the smack lay fast. Toby's face was like a mask, quite expressionless. He was bending on the mainsail while he waited. His eyes went continuously to the tide which now covered the saltings, and a bead of sweat trickled down his nose.

"It must be midnight by now," Emily said. "She must lift!"

"The tide's still making," Toby said.

His calmness, and the smack's stubborn immobility, goaded Emily. She paced up and down the deck angrily, willing the old boat to lift. She thought it felt as if it had died, and was more likely to lie with the water swilling up over the deck than lift to please her. She felt like screaming at it. It was two years since she had been aboard, and she was appalled at the cracked decks, the frayed rigging, and worn blocks. Once *My Alice* had been as shining as a Sunday parlor, trim and strong. She did not know that the smack's condition moved Toby almost to tears, but she had the tact not to put her dismay into words.

"I'll not move the mooring warps until she lifts," Toby said. "There's a chance we might have to go back."

"Go back?" Emily breathed.

She looked down the moon-white water toward the quay. The tall masts and brailed-up sails of two Thames barges dominated the creek, which looked strangely wide in the flood tide. The grass mound of Pewit Island was almost engulfed and the river beyond was full and shining. The west wind, a mere zephyr, scarcely disturbed the flood. Never had it looked to Emily so inviting. The thought of going back was unbearable.

"We'll know in five minutes," Toby said. "She's full now. The smacks are turning."

The smacks that lay at anchor in deep water were beginning to turn athwart the creek, which meant that the tide was on the turn. It was the sign Toby had been dreading. He walked across the deck to shift his weight and perhaps ease her, then picked up one of the long poles that lay on the deck.

"The mud's holding her perhaps. The water's up to her marks. Take the other pole, Emmy, and we'll see if she'll shift."

With a pole each, they prodded for a firm hold and pushed desperately, first from aft, then, to ease the deeper stern, from forward. The smack sighed and, suddenly, from the stern a warp creaked and tautened. Toby looked back, galvanized out of his despair.

"She's moved!" He dropped his pole with a clatter and ran to the stern. With his sheath knife he severed the two warps, and the smack slid forward with a curtsy of her bowsprit to the water. Emily stood breathless, her heart pounding. The smack swung to her anchor and a second bow line brought her up awkwardly in her gentle progress. Toby thrust his knife into Emily's hand and said, "Cut the warp!" He threw himself on the anchor warp. Water and mud flew up over the bows. Emily grasped the hairy warp which was her responsibility and started hacking desperately. Toby's knife was sharp and she had sliced it through before Toby had got in all the mooring warp.

"Can you find the staystail halyard?" he gasped. "Get ready to put the sail up when I shout."

Slimy rope and green weed covered the foredeck. Emily stumbled over it to the mast and looked in despair at the jungle of halyards. She pulled one or two experimentally, then heard the blessed clank of the anchor coming aboard. Toby's calloused hand plucked out the halyard and thrust it into hers.

"Haul away," he said, and darted aft to the tiller.

My Alice was moving. As Toby put the tiller over and the first few feet of sailcloth went hesitantly up the stay, she slid down the hidden channel into deep water. The light wind found the sail, and the smack that had been so lumpen and inert a minute ago now slipped easily through the water, throwing up a chuckle at the bows that sent a shock of triumph through Emily's body. She made fast the staysail halyard and went aft to Toby. He was grinning like a cat.

"I can hear 'em snoring from here!" he said, with a rude gesture toward the village. His purple, closed eye was a positive flag of defiance. Emily smiled uncertainly. She looked down the creek where all the smacks, now lying athwart a slack tide, seemed to be making a barrier across their path. Tody did not seem perturbed. With an inch of the tiller one way and then the other, an eye on his swollen staysail, he threaded *My Alice* through her sisters, shaving bowsprits and sterns with what seemed to Emily incredible luck. Or was it judgment? She was cold with apprehension. The heavy-laden sterns of the Thames barges with their ponderous scrollwork, *Louisa* and *Gregory,* slid past; the sprits reared above the quay like gibbets. A lantern burned on the deck of one, but there was not a living soul to be seen. The village was in darkness, and already Pewit Island was falling away astern.

Emily stared desperately at the familiar sights, the triumph turning to a moment of panic. There was suddenly precious little of the enchantment she had imagined in this moon-lit escape, only a realization that the cutting of the warps in the mud berth back up the creek had meant far more in cold fact than she had ever grasped. This shabby, pitch-soaked, fish-stinking smack was now her home whether she liked it or not. For a moment she thought of asking Toby to put her ashore, then she noticed the cocky tilt of his head and the gleam in his good eye, and the anguish subsided. *My Alice* was free of the fishing boats and dipping to the swell of the open sea.

"Take the tiller," Toby said, "and I'll get the mainsail up."

As her hand took the polished wood she knew she was committed. The certainty calmed her. Toby pulled on the halyards and the gaff swung up, heaving the faded red sail up against the moon where the wind hardened it, pressing out its faded wrinkles.

"Free the mainsheet," Toby called.

The boom swung out as Emily unloosed the coils, and *My Alice* quickened. The water was smooth as glass. The wind scarcely ruffled it, yet it was enough to please the old smack. Emily felt the tiller pull at her hand. The wind was behind them, and she knew she must not let the smack jibe. Instinctively she eased the tiller across to bring the wind more on the beam, and as she did so she remembered her father saying once that she was a "natural." The memory pleased her and the old excitement crept back. She watched the dark shore slipping away, and the flat line of the sea wall where she had walked so often, broken to seaward by the dark shape of the Roman chapel. It might be a long time before she walked there again. The freedom she had always felt there was becoming reality as the smack sailed out to sea.

Toby came back aft, smiling all over his face.

"Luck's with us, eh? We couldn't have had better than this—fair wind and just enough of it. Here, give me the tiller. You can go below and sleep if you like. The old mattresses are still on the bunks."

"Sleep!" Emily had never felt more awake in her life. She settled herself against the hatch coaming, smoothing her skirt which was soaked with splashes from the anchor warp which Toby had now stowed below. Toby said, "Daft clothes for a boat. You'll have to wear dad's old trousers. There's a pair below."

"They'd put me in the mad house." Women weren't supposed to want to run, Emily supposed, and climb down scullery roofs. "What do you think they'll say in the morning when they find out what's happened?"

"I'm hoping they'll be glad to be rid of us," Toby said. "We don't want them to come looking. That's why I thought Southend or Leigh, rather than Colne or Burnham that's closer. Kent might be better still, save that we know someone in Southend."

"You say you do," Emily corrected. "Do you know his name and where he lives?"

"Father called him Will."

"Will what?"

"Just Will. I don't know what. He had a black beard and leather thighboots off a Dutchman. Father asked him to get him a pair of the same."

Emily gave her brother a scornful look. "If that's all you know, we'll be lucky to find him."

"He lived in a row of cottages by the shore, this side of the pier."

"But it must be five—six—years ago since we went there. I reckon it will all be changed now."

"Reckon away then. What does it matter? We'll make a living without his help."

Emily did not think that now was the time to start doubting Toby's confidence, so she turned her attention to the present. They were running off the Mersea shore, well out, heading for the distant Spitway, a gap in the unseen shoals that made the local shores so difficult and dangerous. For most of the journey Emily knew the smack would be out of sight of land. Toby, like all Essex fishermen, regarded the difficulties of the local waters as part of the job: to know the waters, the swatchways and guts where a smack could creep through before half ebb to cut off twenty or so miles of sailing, or find a safe anchorage in bad weather, was equally as important as knowing how to get a stow net full of sprats. To go aground in bad weather on the hard off-shore sands was as fatal to a sailing ship as hitting rock on craggier coasts.

Toby, having spent a larger proportion of his time afloat than ashore during the last six of his sixteen years, knew his way to Southend as surely as any carrier through the lanes. Emily had no doubts as to his competence on that score. With the ebb now running strongly beneath her and the light wind in her sail, *My Alice* was making good progress. The water slapped and leaped under her stem and ran astern past the rowing boat with flickers of phosphorescence jumping like fishes. Emily, half thrilled, half afraid,

watched the brilliance guardedly. She was afraid to think ahead, but could not stop herself. She tried just to look at the water, and eventually the motion overcame her excitement and she dozed. She remembered waking stiffly at dawn, and being conscious of a sun-shot mist all around her and the mainsail hanging like a great dead bird overhead, but Toby said they were all right and she went below and slept again. The next time she awoke the slapping of the water under the old timbers was brisk once more, and the cabin was at an angle. She lifted her head, and felt slightly sick. The strangeness filled her with sadness. She could not believe that this was the beginning of her new life.

But Toby was shouting down to her, his voice full of excitement.

"Emmy! Are you awake! Come up and take an eyeful of our new home port! Southend it is, coming up on the starboard bow now!"

Southend

"Good gracious!" said Emily. "Whatever's that?"

She pushed her hair away out of her eyes and went forward to stand at the shrouds. *My Alice* was beating up into the wind about a mile offshore, and ahead of her, sticking out from the shore, was the longest jetty Emily had ever seen. A paddle steamer was just departing from the end of it: Emily estimated that whoever it had deposited was still a mile from land. Her eyes followed the leggy curiosity to its beginning on shore. A road ran up from it over grassy banks to some handsome buildings that stood on the crown of a hill, looking out to sea. At the bottom of the hill, to the seaward of the pier, was a row of new buildings, houses and taverns by the look of them, whose grassy frontages gave on to shingle beach. Apart from that the prospect was completely unimposing. Having based her ideas of Southend on the picture postcards she had seen of the busy sea fronts and harbors of Ramsgate and Margate, Emily was astounded at the peaceful scene that met her eyes.

"Is that Southend? Is that all?" she said.

"What do you mean, is that all?" Toby said, grinning at her. "That's better than Bradwell quay, isn't it? What more do you want? Bathing machines?"

"Oh, look, there *are* bathing machines," Emily said suddenly. "Three, against the pier."

The first shock over, Emily quickly readjusted her ideas. "Those houses on top of the hill are very handsome, and the new ones going up over there are rather fine. A lovely view they have too." On the far shore, some six miles away, the mouth of the river Medway could be seen converging with the Thames, and the Isle of Sheppey in its mouth and the Kent coast showed up clear and blue in the morning sun. Westward, inland, the estuary narrowed, and the brown topsail of a Thames barge could be seen above the glint of marshes. It was not the only sail to be seen either. A tea clipper was coming down, making use of the westerly wind to stem the tide, and the auxiliary sails of a steamboat could be seen against Sheppey, making into the Medway. Inshore several small fishing boats were working, and Toby was far more interested in the motley fleet than in the beauty of the clipper.

"Look, she's going to China," Emily said.

"That's a bawley, Emmy," Toby said. "That one off the end of the pier. See, there's a few of 'em beyond. It's the local fishing boat—different from a smack, isn't she?"

"Fatter," Emily agreed. "Heavier."

"That's what we want if we settle here."

Emily said nothing. She was full of such a mixture of excitement and fear, and happiness and light, and fear again, that she daren't put any more into words. Each tack brought *My Alice* nearer to the fantastic pier, where Emily could now see ladies walking and a horse drawing a carriage along, presumably to collect the passengers who had disembarked from the paddle steamer. Up the hill beyond the pier a young wood was bursting into leaf under the noses of the elegant houses, misting the haphazard shore with green. Trees and bushes grew in a tangle to the shore, holding the slipping sandy cliffs back from the sea.

"Take the tiller. I'll see we're ready to put the anchor over," Toby ordered.

Toby took *My Alice* up close to the pier and let out the anchor fairly close to the shore.

"She'll dry out here when the tide falls," he said when the sails were stowed and the boat was riding calmly to her warp. "I'll have a bit of a sleep and then we'll have a look around."

"See if we can find Will with Dutch boots on," said Emily with faint derision.

"Aye. They seem to have planted some grand new homes where those fishermen's cottages were," Toby said, glancing at the shore. "But I'll worry about that later."

He yawned. When he had gone below Emily ate her share of the pie that he had left her, wrapped her shawl around her, and sat on the deck to absorb her new home. The afternoon was mild. The tide was ebbing, revealing the gawky timber legs of the pier and a vast expanse of dimpled mud and sand. By four o'clock *My Alice* was lying over and Toby, turning in his sleep, fell out of his bunk onto the floor. He came up on deck, blinking. Emily looked at him gratefully. She felt she had been a long time alone.

"Shall we go ashore now?" she asked eagerly, scrambling to her feet. She had put her hair up and scraped the mud off her skirt. "We've time to look at the houses before it goes dark."

"I'd rather look at the boats," Toby said, gazing around at the various fishing craft that had come in while he had been asleep and now lay scattered on the mud all around them like stranded crabs.

"Oh, come on," Emily said. "They can't go away. Let's see if we can find this Will you've been talking about. We haven't a penny till we either find him or earn some."

"Oh, haven't we?" said Toby. He put a hand in his pocket and pulled out two sovereigns, which he held out to her on his palm.

"Wherever did you get those from?" Emily gasped. "You never stole them?"

"No, I did not," Toby said, putting them away again. He flushed slightly. "It felt like it at the time. I found them in our father's jacket when he died, and I took them before anyone else did. I've had them ever since."

"But, Toby, that's splendid! I thought we hadn't a penny. We won't starve for a bit."

"What do you mean, for a bit?" Toby growled. "Here, I shall have to carry you ashore. You've no shoes for the mud."

He swung himself over the stern and climbed down over the rudder, and Emily followed, slithering onto his shoulders and riding precariously to the hard shingle.

"Lucky you're skinny," he said, dropping her with a grunt. It had been quite a walk. They stood and looked out across the shining ebb, where the late afternoon sun was turning mud to gold and water to silver with ravishing abandon. The Kentish shore was hazy and indistinct, like another country. A pair of steam tugs crawled like beetles past Sheerness, etching their smoke on the colorless sky, and collier brigs with sails of gold leaf drifted on the last of the ebb. On the edge of the mud the cocklers were working with their rakes and mud sledges, and some boys were splashing under the pier looking for oysters.

Toby and Emily walked across the shore to examine the houses that faced the sea. They were elegant and impressive, but it wasn't difficult to discern traces of the more inelegant and unimpressive buildings they had replaced. Here and there, squashed between bright new bricks, were ramshackle boat sheds and a wooden cottage or two. Toby asked the most likely looking man they met if he knew anything of "Will," but it wasn't until he had inquired of a fifth man that he got any information.

"I reckon you mean Will Porter—him that was drowned in sixty-four. Big fellow with a big black beard? Aye. He lived down here one time."

"He was drowned?"

"Aye."

Toby inquired no further. The details were of no interest, only the fact that the man no longer existed to give them help or advice. He looked at Emily, rather shamefaced.

"Well, that's him then."

"You said it wouldn't matter," Emily pointed out. "It won't have to matter now."

They walked up the hill toward what they gathered was thought of at the bottom of the hill as "the new town." Above the bright budding of the young trees the Royal Hotel faced the sea proudly; it had the air of sophistication and plush that Emily had dreamed of. Standing on a corner, it divided the terrace of handsome houses that faced the sea from the High Street that ran inland. But the High Street, which Emily had based on vague memories of Colchester, was a distinct disappointment. It did not end in a square with a Renaissance town hall or Gothic cathedral, but petered out quite soon into a lane that went meandering away unpurposefully amongst trees and fields. On either side roads ran off where a lot of new houses were being built. If Southend was up and coming, it had not yet, in Emily's opinion, arrived.

"Bradwell's as busy as this," Toby agreed as, having walked as far as the end of the High Street and looked at the empty railway station, they made their way back to the top of the hill. Emily thought he exaggerated, but agreed with his general disappointment.

"Of course, it's busier here in the summer," she pointed out. "It's not a port, like Bradwell, it's a summer place for people to come to."

"I saw Margate from the smack once, and Margate's a hundred times bigger than this," Toby said.

"Well, London people have always gone to Margate, on the steamer," Emily said. "They don't come here the same. Only people who like it quiet."

"The steamers have always landed easy at Margate, that's the difference," Toby said. "It grew up early and got its name before Southend got a pier built. And the tide doesn't go out so far the other side. That mud and sand down there is the Maplins, Emmy. All right at high water, but look at it on the ebb!"

They stood on the top of the hill and looked out across the shining estuary. The water broke in a thread of gold far out by the end of the pier, and from there to the shore, more than a mile wide, the shining acres of shoal sand and mud known as the Maplins blazed like fire in the light of the setting sun. Beyond, out in deep water, sails drifted home; there was no wind. Emily looked at it fiercely, aware of the beauty, but holding the pleasure away from her. This was their adventure at its best. She knew that, just as the sun was going to set and the scene change to cold, smelly mud and a sullen tide, their adventure was about to change from excitement and novelty to something far more prosaic and uncomfortable and insecure. A pang of homesickness rose up in her like a pain. She couldn't tell if her eyes were watering with tears or with the sun.

"Come on. We'll buy some bread and get back aboard," Toby said. "I'll go around and find out what I can about the fishing and the market here. It's no good catching the stuff if I can't sell it afterwards."

They bought bread and cheap dripping and some watery ale, collected a bundle of driftwood for the stove, and went back to *My Alice*. She was still lying over uncomfortably. Toby ate some bread and dripping and went off on his explorations, and Emily lit a couple of candles and surveyed her new home.

My Alice's cuddy was a black pit forward of the mast, with no place for light to enter save down the hatch. It was tiny, narrowing forward so that the two narrow bunks, one on either side, almost met at the heads. At the foot of the steps down from the deck an ancient black stove was wedged with its back to the mast and a leaky chimney reached up through the roof. The deck timbers were so low that it was impossible to stand up; only by sitting on the bunks was one able to shuffle about without getting a crick in one's neck. Apart from one small, evil-smelling locker, there was nowhere to put anything. Anything, apart from Emily's bundle, consisted of three chipped mugs, a few odd pieces of cutlery, a water cask, a bucket, and a damp blanket to each bunk. The mattresses on the bunks were covered with mildew and mice from the saltings had been at them. Their straw filling shed at every movement. Immediately aft of the cuddy was the fish-hold, whose flavor permeated the whole thirty-foot length of the smack. The fish, Emily realized, had far more room to move about in than she had. She did not see how she was ever to make this dank hole into a home. She sat in the half-darkness, trying to remember that this was freedom and independence, and wondering what the Boots had said when they discovered that their slaves had vanished. Neither reflection gave her any consolation.

My Alice had lifted and was afloat by the time Toby came back, smelling of beer and very cheerful. He had been ferried out from the shore by a boy whom he introduced to Emily as Dick. Emily saw in the darkness a still darker head, and a gleam of gypsy-like eyes as the boy said, "Pleased to meet you, miss."

"I'll see you tomorrow then, Dick," Toby said.

"Aye."

Emily, furiously indignant to see Toby so apparently sated with pleasure while she had endured such a miserable evening contemplating the cuddy, turned on him as soon as the boy had rowed away and said sharply, "You've been drinking!"

"Where else would I meet a fisherman this time of night but in a tavern?" Toby said equably.

The honest truth of the reply calmed Emily, who had thought Toby was on the road to ruin within twenty-four hours of leaving home.

"Oh, and what did you find out?"

"I met that boy Dick you saw. He told me quite a bit, all I wanted to know. He said he'll sort out gear with me tomorrow and I can sail with him—he's got a dad who's a fisherman—and all his brothers. They've got three bawleys between them. He said I can take my catches into Leigh with them, and he knows a boy who might sail with me—" Toby's words ended in an enormous yawn. "I did all right, Emmy. Things aren't so bad at all." He clattered down the companionway and threw himself on the bunk and fell asleep within the minute.

Emily stayed up on deck for a few moments, looking at the lights shining up on the hill. In the cool, windless dark, sounds carried clearly from the shore: the rumble of carriage wheels up the hill, the singing and shouting from one of the new inns, probably the one where Toby had been. Dim, curtained lights shone from the windows of the elegant terrace she had explored earlier, to be answered out across the estuary by the stronger, urgent flashes of the

lightship and, distantly, by a flicker from the ships anchored
in the mouth of the Medway. The pier was lit, and under its
wooden piles the tide echoed, hollow and sad, filling up the
cocklers' trails and smoothing the trodden mud. A smell of
seaweed and sewage, of spring in the trees and fish in the
hold, mingled in Emily's nose.

She went below. Toby lay on his back with all his clothes
on, even his boots. He was smiling in his sleep. Emily sniffed
and threw the blanket over him, then undressed carefully
(and with considerable difficulty, being unable to stand up),
put on her nightdress, and lay down on the knobbly mattress. Soon she got up again and put on her woolen jacket
and her stockings and added her shawl to the blanket. And
slept.

Emily's home was on the water, whether she liked it or
not, but her heart was centered on the new, prosperous,
serene buildings ashore. She could not help Toby; girls
could not go fishing. On the boat she was so much ballast,
in the way on deck and seasick below, but on shore there
was work for her somewhere. She was quick and intelligent.
Somebody would give her a straw mattress and her keep
for her help in their kitchen, or their shop, or their tavern,
she felt sure. It was difficult keeping her clothes uncrum-
pled and clean in the poky cuddy, and she wanted to find
herself a place before she lost what she realized was bound
to be a losing battle with her respectability. With work,
she could start saving her pennies toward the cottage. She
was glad that living with the Boot family had made her
hard and able to take knocks and abuse; she liked to think
that she could boldly talk her way into a place where she
chose. When Toby landed her on the shingle beach, however, she was trembling inside and sick with a mixture of

wild optimism and anxiety, and it was difficult to feel as bold as she was convinced she was. Toby gave her a queer, compassionate look.

"What are you going to do?"

"I'll try the hotel and the taverns first, and see if they want a kitchenmaid."

"You don't want a rough place, remember. It's something decent you want."

"Well, of course," she said lamely. She felt worse at the way Toby looked at her. People were walking and riding along the strand above the beach, the cockle-gatherers were making for home with their baskets of shellfish, a woman was going shopping, a boy was delivering meat. She looked at them enviously. They all belonged, and had a place, even the raggedest of the cockling boys. She felt as conspicuous starting on her errand as a ten-foot giant, or a woman with two heads. She knew where she was going, of course, but she felt far from bold as she came to the doorway of the Royal Hotel. Her heart was banging at her ribs and her cheeks burned with embarrassment. In her confusion she almost walked in at the front door, but the sight of the thick red carpet beneath her muddy shoe brought her to her senses, and she searched out the back entrance down an alley and found a boy putting empty bottles in a crate.

"What d'you want?" he asked, as she stood there, hesitating and tongue-tied.

"Is—can—can I see the cook?"

"She a friend of yours?"

"No. I—I want a job."

"You're not the only one, are you?" the boy said glumly. "There's no jobs here I know of. Go and ask her. News to me if there is."

Emily went to the back door, but a man in a waiter's

suit was standing there. He said there were no jobs and stared at her closely in an ignorant, curious way that was soon to become familiar.

"Where do you come from?" he asked.

The question came as a surprise and Emily could think of no answer. She was afraid to say Bradwell, and could hardly cite a smack as a home, even if it were the truth. Her loss for an answer increased her discomfort. She stammered, and lied, "Maldon, sir."

"There's hotels in Maldon. Better try at home," the waiter said. "There's not much work here this time of the year."

A flat disappointment cooled Emily's flushed face. She went back down the hill without any pleasure in the blue sky and the great plate of the almost blue estuary shimmering below her. She called at the three new hotels—the Minerva, the Middleton, the Army and Navy—and the old Ship, to receive brusque or indifferent refusals from all four. The four refusals were like four slaps in the face, but hesitancy gave way to stubbornness. There were more places than inns, anyway. There were shops, and rich people's houses in the new Cliff Town roads where servants would be needed, and perhaps sewing. Emily dared not knock on doors to inquire after a job as a housemaid, but she summoned up the courage to ask shop people, and cooks doing their shopping, and bakers' boys. But Southend was a small place; the population was little over two thousand. Emily was a stranger and the fact made her conspicuous. During the next few days she found she was asking the same baker's boy again, and the cooks smiled at her in a way she suspected was pitying, and any lady of the house she ever had the good fortune to meet face to face invariably asked her for references, and shook her head when she said she hadn't any. "Little thief, more than likely," she once heard a woman remark to her husband before she was out of earshot.

It soon became evident that there were a lot more girls in Southend besides herself wanting places, and generally they had a sister, or a brother who already worked somewhere where there was a place going. When she tried for sewing, she found that in the gown shop there were already two long rows of pale-faced girls stitching away at the new straight-fronted skirts. The proprietor told her that the sudden decease of the crinoline and the new fashion of the bustle was giving him a great deal of work, but apparently he did not consider it a reason for taking on more girls. Judging from the appearance of the ones he already had, Emily concluded that it would have been more accurate to state that the new fashion was giving the girls a lot more work and the proprietor a lot more money. She did not envy the sewing drudges. She was offered cut shirts to sew at home, but as the pay was only tenpence halfpenny for a dozen and they would no doubt smell of fish when she had finished, she turned down the offer.

Meanwhile, her "home" spent most of each day out in the estuary, generally out of sight, and the fact that Toby was actually earning his first money of his own was the only comfort that Emily had. There was precious little else. She spent hours wandering up and down the beach waiting for him to come home, or sheltering in Dick's grandmother's hovel—it was little more—when she got too cold. Only desperation drove her there, for Dick's grandmother was old and deaf and filthy and always sent her out for gin. When she felt the familiar despair mounting, Emily would set her teeth and make herself think of Mark, and

Toby's black eye, and Gideon Boot's harsh voice, and Aunt Mary's shrill scolding. To dwell for even a moment on the white rose bush or even Bradwell's homely village street was to invite hot tears of self-pity which, once started, were very hard to stop. Emily convinced herself that she was glad they had come, but the conviction was very shaky. And with each day that passed she felt herself becoming more the girl that the prosperous women who asked for references obviously thought she was. Her thin shoes were getting cracked with the mud, her skirt stained, all her clothes smelling of the wood smoke that belched out of the cracked stove every night and the whitebait that filled the hold by day. The salt was in her hair and it clung in a thick sticky bundle to the back of her head. She was invariably hungry and terrified, when she loitered, of being apprehended, asked for her address, and landing up in the workhouse. When Toby came home, late and eager, she tried to take comfort in his achievement, but the long disheartening day had generally extinguished even her last flicker of enthusiasm.

"Never mind, Emmy. In a week or two, if I go on like this, you won't have to work. I'll pay for a cottage." Toby was as full of hope as Emily was depressed. He tried to cheer her up, but Emily knew that for months to come any penny he earned would have to be put into old *My Alice,* who was scarcely fit to sail in anything but a zephyr and sadly short of gear. He also had Dick's cousin to pay for his help. Dick sailed with his father and elder brother on a large bawley called *Content.* Although Dick was now Toby's fast friend, and his father had lent him nets and rope, Emily instinctively disliked the family. The father, Alf Harvey, was a burly, ignorant man who drank all his takings and sent his wife out cockling to pay the rent, and Dick was not what Emily called a steady boy. He was seventeen, and had black hair, tightly curling, and very dark brown eyes, wide brawling shoulders, and an aggressive tilt to his chin. To Emily, he looked the very personification of a bad influence, although she had to admit that he was kind and seemed good-natured enough. He had certainly gotten Toby started, tagging him onto the little family fleet, which unloaded its catch every night on the end of the pier. Toby had more than the two sovereigns jangling in his pocket now and said happily to Emily, "We'll have new shrouds by the end of the month."

Emily had just come down from the deck, where she had stayed as long as possible watching a strange red-velvet sun sinking down into a bank of stormy purple streamers over the marshes. The glare had touched the proud houses on the hill with an unearthly brilliance, and Emily had imagined that their feverishly lit window eyes had been mocking at her for her humble efforts to get into their basement kitchens. The cliff and the shore, and the black spider legs of the pier had looked impossibly romantic and remote to Emily, who felt as chained to her uncomfortable home afloat as a convict on a prison hulk. An easterly wind was chopping up the sea so that the smack pitched uneasily. Emily hated the motion below in the black cuddy, and huddled on the bunk watching a pan of small herrings sizzling on top of the stove. The stench of fish and damp, smoking wood, the uneasy slap of water in the bilges, the hazy light of the oil lamp were all as familiar to her now as Aunt Mary's kitchen. The incessant crick in her back and neck from stooping was her new occupational disease. So was the seasickness in her stomach.

"Where did you go today?" Toby asked, giving the herrings a shake around. The pungent, greasy smell and the heaving of the straw mattress beneath her made Emily bite her lip. She replied briefly, "Nowhere."

"You been everyhere now then?"

"I daren't go anywhere decent looking like this," Emily looked down at her mud-caked hem and split shoes.

Toby's face clouded over. He opened his mouth, then shut it again, changing his mind.

"Wind's getting up," he said noncommittally. The pan slid across the top of the stove and he caught it neatly. "They're done now. Pass the plates."

"I couldn't eat any," Emily said, shuddering.

"Do you good," Toby said. "A full stomach's good for sickness."

Emily shook her head, her lips tightly shut. Toby started to eat out of the pan, wedging it between his knees. Emily tried not to look. *My Alice* plunged and groaned, and the anchor warp creaked in the fairlead. Halyards and blocks tapped and jerked and the tiller moved backward and forward with a restless, rhythmic groan that set Emily's teeth on edge. She put her head in the mildewed straw and willed herself to bear it. If you can bear this, her mind ran, you can bear anything. The smoke, the damp, the pit of the cuddy that was her home, and outside a storm-sharp cliff looking like something out of an old painting—all hectic streaks of light from the dregs of the sunset—all represented, at that moment, unendurable misery. She clenched her fists and pushed her nose into the straw to shut out the hot herrings. Toby ate steadily, an anxious eye on her. When he had finished he put the pan down and went on deck to check the anchor warp before it got dark.

"Come and look at this, Emmy!"

Emily groaned to herself.

"It's worth it!" the inexorable voice goaded her. Toby was standing in the hatch, and Emily groped her way to the foot of the companionway. "What is it?"

"What a night! Come and look. And this old packet beating across—she'll be aground if she doesn't watch it."

Toby's legs moved on up out of the hatch and a weird light shone down on Emily's face. She climbed up and looked out. *My Alice* was lying well offshore; the tide, two hours ebbed, had not yet left her, and the restless water all around her was shining with an unearthly lurid light. The darkening sky was greenish and purple like a great bruise. Beating down the river, a big ketch was standing in, close-hauled, toward the edge of the sands, apparently anxious to catch her tide out into deep water. Emily had never seen so big a ship so close inshore before, and caught her breath at the sight of the lean bows hissing into the swell and the bare topmasts etched against the storm-bellied sky. It was so close that the orders to go about carried clearly to Emily and Toby as they stood watching.

"And none too soon!" Toby breathed. "I reckon they've got a drunken captain aboard that ship. Or pilot, or both."

The lean bows bore away, plunging through clouds of flying spray. Emily saw a purplish, ragged ensign, and the angry flurry of broken water on the edge of the shoal, spray blowing off the wave tops.

"The wind's going to the southeast," Toby said. "If she's going up the Swin she should have it fair beyond Shoebury. But he's cutting it fine, by God! I reckon they're drunk aboard."

"But surely it is a passenger ship!"

"No. She's a trading ketch, but she might have a few passengers aboard. There's not many passengers will go by sail now when they can go on a steamboat."

"I wouldn't like to be in that one." Emily looked out again, cautiously. The pier lights were blurred with rain, a fine, horizontally driving rain that soon made her duck once more. Toby, careless of the weather, stood looking down the river estuary. Half a dozen bawleys were heading for the pierhead, too late to get into Leigh, and a steamboat passed, bowling upriver with its auxiliary sail giving it far more speed than its engines. But the great rain-blurred estuary otherwise was bare and ominous. Toby did not like the look of it at all, nor did he think highly of his own situation, although he would not tell Emily that. There was no shelter at Southend from a southeasterly, and he had the pier on his lee, which would do him no good if his anchor dragged. When they went aground, the smack would take a hammering before she was left high and dry, and he thought a good deal of her caulking would very likely fall out, a prospect which did nothing to cheer him. He put his head down the hatch again.

"Listen, Emmy, I'm going to move. We'll go up and see if there's any room for us in Leigh gut. It's not a good place here if it's going to blow."

Emily's heart sank.

"Do you want any help?"

Toby hesitated. He didn't want to call her out; on the other hand, they were uncomfortably close to the pier. Two more hands might make all the difference.

"Just to get under way. Then you can get into your bunk and sleep it out."

Emily forgot her sickness in the blinding chill of the rain

and the acute misery of keeping her feet on the pitching deck. Toby got some reefed rags of sails up and cleared the pier end by a boat's length. The unloading bawleys gave them a wave and a shout, and as Toby headed *My Alice's* bowsprit up the river, Emily pulled her hair back out of her eyes and made for the hatch. She put her foot on the companionway, and as she did so a strange red light suddenly glossed the sky. Thinking it was some phenomenon of the weather she looked around in fright.

"A distress signal!" Toby shouted.

Over Shoeburyness a red flare hung in the sky, lighting the sky and the water with a ghastly sheen. Emily heard the report, faintly, and stopped in her tracks. Already Toby had put the tiller over to put the smack about.

"It'll be that ketch!" he shouted excitedly. "What did I tell you? She stood in too far, or hit the Barrow!"

"What are we going to do?" Emily shouted, as the mainsail cracked over and Toby started hauling in the sheet. Water poured across the decks and slopped over her bare ankles as she came back out of the hatch. She was crying, because she knew what Toby was going to do, but in the storm and the flarelight her emotions were of no importance. She knew it. She wiped her face and went back aft to Toby.

"Look, those bawleys are making off too," Toby said. "We might be able to do something." He looked at Emily sternly. "I'll land you at the pier if you want."

"Oh, no! It'll waste too much time."

"Go and get my jersey and smock on you then. There'll be hard work ahead."

Emily did as she was told.

The Ketch in Trouble

My Alice was not alone, pitching into the steep seas off the Maplins. Most of the boats which were not aground had sailed off and, as if in support, lights were moving along the shore. Emily could imagine doors opening, and the taverns emptying, the men brought curiously to the shore. The bawleys, as quick off the pierhead as Toby, were just ahead of *My Alice* and their presence comforted Emily. She needed comfort, for the situation they were in appalled her. She had never sailed in rough weather before, and the thought of the wreck ahead petrified her.

What did Toby suppose he was going to do, she wondered. One glance at his face told her that he had none of her doubts: it was alive with an eagerness that amazed her. He stood at the tiller completely oblivious to the weather, oblivious to her, his whole mind with the straining smack as she pitched into the lumpy, driving waves. There was an authority about him that Emily had never sensed before. It was as if he were his father in that moment, a being Emily had never questioned nor doubted. She was comforted again, and the panic gave way to a grim sense of duty. If Toby could react like that to the emergency, the least she could do was keep her head and try not to be sick.

She put an old stinking smock over her clothes, bound
her flying hair up with a scarf, and stood in the companionway, her legs warm with the fire below and her face stinging in the rain. She had to brace herself to keep in place. The
old smack was crashing into the steep seas with a violence
that Emily thought would shake her to bits. In fact, their
own peril seemed to her every bit as dire as the wreck they
were heading for. When she looked alongside at their com-
panions, she saw their rakish bowsprits plunging into the

waves like great harpoons to disappear for long seconds at
a time, while the water ran up along the decks like a vicious
animal, swilling its white teeth around the hatch covers and
the boots of their crew. And she knew how *My Alice* looked
to them and how she must look, clinging to the hatch
coaming with her hands red and raw and wet and the spray
hissing onto the stove below. It was dark, and yet the sky
was lit by a strange greenish glare from the west, so that
the wave tops could be seen crusting the water far out into
the estuary and seething along the edge of the Maplins. The
savage beauty of it haunted Emily; she was afraid but exhilarated by it. She had never looked a storm in the face
before.

"Can you see the wreck?" she shouted at Toby.

"I can see a light," he shouted back. "I reckon she's on
the Oaze, or hit that wreck that's lying there!"

Emily shivered. What was Toby going to do, she kept
thinking. Were there men in the water over there? She
looked closely at the water where it broke and tossed and
grinned at her over the wallowing bulwarks. She thought
of a man in it, his face turning up for air and the wave
breaking down on him. How did you swim in such a
sea? Emily could not swim, although she knew Toby could.
Did the waves carry you up, as they carried up *My Alice,*
and dash you down in their troughs as the old smack fell,
cracking her stem in the bottom as if it were stone?

Toby was shouting something to the nearest bawley.
Emily heard a voice shout back, full of excitement. She did
not hear the words, but she knew that the men were enjoying themselves, Toby as well. She guessed, from what
she knew, that they stood to gain from a weck: the mercy

dash was more than a show of humanity. The dark sails were more like the wings of the carrion crows, she thought, in for the pickings. Out beyond the bawleys, she could see a small boat making as if from the Kent coast, a smack-type yacht with a black hull, fast and shapely beside the bawleys. She went past the fishing boats and Emily heard the men swearing about her as she showed them her heels. They swore because she was going to get there first. Emily, who was thinking of the people who were perhaps even now drowning, looked contemptuously at the bawley men.

It was a long, hard beat to the wreck. Emily, sick and scared, lost all sense of time, conscious only of the whine of the wind and the groaning of the smack's frayed rigging. She knew without Toby telling her that the shrouds were likely to part and the mast come down at any moment; she could see Toby's face puckered with anxiety as he stood braced at the tiller. The lights of the wreck were growing nearer, tack by tack, and Emily kept fancying she could hear shouts and screams. In her mind there were shouts and screams and pale drowned faces all around her, but in reality only the flickering light to guide them, uncertain now.

"I reckon we might be too late," Toby was saying.

Emily went and stood beside him, shivering.

"What shall we do?"

"Wait and see. How do I know yet?"

"What are the others going to do? Go aboard her?"

"I dare say. See what there is."

"You won't?"

"No, more's the pity. I can't leave you alone on the smack. We might pick up some poor devils though."

Two more tacks saw the smack close up to the dull light and they strained their eyes into the half-darkness, sailing close-hauled toward the shoal. Other moving lights were their fellow fishing boats, but the still, dull light was a lantern lashed to the aftermast of the ketch. Her dark shape, the unnatural underneath lines of her bilge and keel stood up out of the breaking seas at an agonizing angle. She was as if speared, having run onto the wreck of a brig that had gone aground during the winter. The two wrecks, old and new, were locked together like fighting stags, and with the ebbing of the tide the ketch was crushing the old brig she lay on; the groaning of timbers reached out across the water with a desolation that set Emily's nerves quivering. It was as human as any cry for help she had imagined earlier. The ketch's foremast had snapped off, and sail and rigging spilled in a great moving flotsam in the water, tethered still to the cumbrous, splitting hull. With the yellow waves bursting savagely into the wreckage, the spitted ketch was a miserable sight, a scab of incompetence on the shoal.

Toby put *My Alice* about nervously, clear of the danger, and they went by, staring for any signs of life. The bawleys, Emily noticed, were putting men off in their rowing skiffs to board the wreck, and the black smack-yacht was anchored off in deep water with a light aboard, but apparently deserted. Whoever sailed her had certainly been first aboard. Of drowned crew there was no sign, and the only cries were those of the ship itself, a splitting and sighing of timbers strained beyond endurance.

Emily, shocked but thankful, said, "We've come here for nothing."

Even as she said it a dark figure appeared on the rail of the ketch that was high out of the water and looked across at them. He shouted something, but what it was they couldn't make out.

"Run in close," Emily said. "He could jump down on our deck."

"God, and add *My Alice* to the wreckage?" Toby said.

But he went about again, and hauled in his mainsheet. The dark figure moved to the stern of the ketch and shouted again.

"He says it's safe to run close there!" Emily said.

"Ah, what does he know!" Toby said, white with anxiety. But he had already made up his mind to go. "He'll kill himself," he added angrily.

He took *My Alice* in close-hauled and put her about as near to the wreck as he dared. It was close enough for a nimble man to jump, if he had the courage; Toby was making an offer. The dark figure above them hurtled into their shrouds like a monkey and landed feet first on deck. It was obvious that he was as at home aloft as he was below, and Toby looked at him with respect as he came back aft, holding on to the hatch.

"I've heard of you Southend sharks," he said in a rough, hoarse voice, "but by God, I never thought I'd have dealings with you. If you want to save some lives get down tide and see if there are any poor devils left to pick up out of a lifeboat that capsized. But if you're here for your own good get your anchor down before your friends up there have had it all. I wouldn't like to stand in your way."

His voice was scathing. He braced himself against the hatch and stared at Toby and—with an obvious start of surprise—at Emily.

"God, you're only a couple of kids! And a girl too! Those wretches out there—"

Toby, stung, retorted, "If they're still alive, we'll pick

them up. Go up forward and keep a lookout, Emily. We've not come out here to plunder."

His voice was far from childlike. The man's expression changed and he said, "I'll not judge you by the other then. I told him about the lifeboat and, cool as you please, he said, 'They'll be drowned now, if it's as you say.' There's a girl lying up there on deck with her neck broken by the foremast. The captain's daughter she was. And your Southend gentleman took her necklace off and put it in his pocket, big blue opals like a string of bird's eggs, and he said to me, 'I'll take you ashore when I'm through. Don't worry,' he said. Nice as you like, and his dirty thieving hand still in his pocket and the girl crushed there. 'Don't worry,' he said. Well, I come and get my own lift ashore and pray God you're not all the same as him. Get along now if you're here to be useful. There were women and children in that lifeboat. They had a lantern aboard but it went out suddenly and I heard screams and a shout and damn all since."

The horrors were real enough after all. Emily made her way to the shrouds to act as lookout, filled with a cold dread of what their smack's wild bow wave might turn up, for a moment, on its crest. The sailor was up forward. Emily felt sick. She thought they had been spared the horrors and that Toby could have eased *My Alice* and run her home before the wind with the solitary survivor to make good their trouble. And the danger would have been over and their consciences salved. The thin shrouds quivered beneath her fingers.

"To starboard! To starboard!" The screech jerked Emily into life. She scrambled across the deck and braced herself against the forehatch beside the man off the ketch. She could see nothing. The man was shouting at Toby and

Emily saw Toby hauling in his mainsheet and the sail quivering as she was pinched into the wind.

"No more!" Toby shouted.

"As you are now!"

Emily heard a shout from the water and stared frantically for what their survivor had spotted. A pale bundle of what looked like floating rags rolled on a crest and swung down towards them. The man from the ketch snatched up the hitcher and, bracing himself in the shrouds, thrust the hook out toward the flotsam. He had only one chance. Toby could get the smack no closer on the present tack. Emily lay across the bulwarks and stretched out her arm as the hitcher groped, and held. A spar reared out of the water and thudded heavily against the side of the smack. On it was the pale streaming bundle that Emily could see now was a woman, within reach for that brief moment. With one hand she clutched the spar and with the other she held a child against it. The child, Emily thought, was drowned, but the woman had lifted up her head and her face was red and she screamed with a vigor that Emily herself could not have equaled just then. They knocked and thudded along the side of the smack, but the smack was still sailing and as Emily grasped the woman's clothes around her neck the weight nearly pulled her overboard. She gasped as her sockets creaked, and heard the man beside her cry out, "Hold her! Hold her!" She alone, aching and panting, held the screaming dead weight as he fetched the hitcher inboard and snatched up a warp from the foredeck. Toby ran up forward and the two men at last took the woman's weight.

"Leave the child!" the man said, but Emily thrust down and caught the thin arm, and could not let it go. The spar floated away, and beneath the flogging mainsail the two men struggled with the woman against the counter, slipping and swearing. With her heavy waterlogged clothes and her hysterics she was almost more than they could manage, and Emily knew that the child was her responsibility alone if she was stupid enough to struggle with it. It was quite limp, face-down in the water. Emily had its arm and lay across the bulwarks trying to summon up the strength to lift it. Its clothes pulled it down like weeds. The smack rolled and almost rolled Emily under, and the water poured beneath her down the bulwarks, but her one red hand held the shrouds and the other the child, and neither would give way.

"You're a fool," she muttered. "It's dead." She was completely unaware of what was going on around her, of the men on the counter or the lights of the other bawleys that had come to search, and the shouts that echoed dully down the tide. She wanted the child on board, if only to make sure it was dead. She was frozen and soaked and stubborn, no longer caring for anything more the storm could do. She pulled the cold arm, and a wave came suddenly and lifted the little body up, and in that moment Emily let go the shrouds and got both arms under the child while it was lifted up beside the bulwarks. And before the water fell away she had got its shoulders over the bulwarks, and she held it by the scruff of the neck and got her knees down against the capping rail and as the smack rolled she heaved again, desperately. The child inside its waterlogged serge was a thin stick of a five-year-old, yet it was all Emily could do to roll the bundle over onto the deck. She rolled with it, exhausted, and lay panting, her own skirts in a wet, clogging mess all about her trembling legs so that she could scarcely move.

The child was a girl. It had a blue-white skin and closed eyes and a thin pale fringe clinging to its forehead. Emily could feel no breath and no pulse, but when she had got her own breath back she heaved herself onto the hatch cover and held the body head down over her knees and beat it on the back to clear the water out of its lungs. She could faintly remember her mother doing that to half-drowned infant Toby one day after he had fallen off the quay and been fished out with a boat hook. But Toby had screamed, and this child lay still. An eyelid flickered. Emily stared at it closely. Or did it? She leaned over it, holding the puppet-like bundle to keep it from rolling off the hatch with the pitching of the smack. She felt like picking it up again and shaking life into it, after the effort it had cost her to pick it out of the sea. She did not feel compassion for it; the stubbornness with which she had held on to it had not left her.

"You will breathe, you little bundle! I'll do it for you," she muttered.

She put her face down close to the white face of the child and breathed into its nostrils. She had heard her father say once that it was the way to revive a drowned child but whether it was just an old sailor's yarn or not she did not know. Her warm breath on the cold face was the only warmth in the whole universe, she felt. She was amazed that there was any warmth in her. She willed it into the child, braced stiff-legged to keep herself in place, her wet hair falling into a tangle like seaweed over the child. Someone shook her roughly by the shoulder but she did not look up. The child gave a little moan. Emily put both hands under its head and lifted it up and saw the nostrils quiver with breath of their own. There was a gasp and a

cry and the bundle was suddenly a living, conscious girl, with a crumpled, reddening face. Emily, looking at the ugly, bawling little thing with an overwhelming sense of relief and pride, felt as if her own life had gone into it. She was exhausted, and scarcely had the strength to pull the child close and comfort her.

The motion of the smack seemed easier, and when she gathered her wits together and looked about her, Emily realized that *My Alice* was running for home. The lights of the bawleys that had anchored or were still beating to the wreck were away over the port quarter and almost lost behind the waves. Toby was at the tiller but there were three men crouched beside him, and from the cuddy below came a noise of sobbing and chattering that Emily could hear even above the crashing of the smack. Obviously they had picked up other survivors while she had been occupied with the child. She knew she should take the child below out of the cold, but she shrank from facing the distress and the babble. Then it struck her that the sight of the child, alive, would at least alleviate its mother's troubles, and she picked the child up with the last of her strength and stumbled with her to the cuddy hatch.

One guttering candle mercifully gave too dull a light for Emily to make out any details. She was aware of two moaning women, more concerned with acute seasickness than with their past adventures and probably wishing they had been left to drown, and a man who told her that the child belonged to neither of the two women, but was the daughter of the captain's daughter. Having already learned the fate of the captain's daughter, Emily took the child on her knee and took off her wet clothes and wrapped her tenderly in her own shawl. She was past emotion, and, huddled in the corner of her bunk with the child in her arms, she fell asleep.

Emily the Housemaid

The woman in the carriage shouted to her coachman to stop, leaned forward, and flung open the door.

"Get in," she said peremptorily to the bedraggled woman that stood nearest. "I'll take the women. Get in."

Her voice was so commanding that the babble among the crowd of people on the beach stopped abruptly. Half the population of the waterfront was there waiting to see what the bawleys brought home, and was making a night out of it. Lanterns flared and sparked across the shore and the few survivors, having struggled the weary way ashore across the mud, were trailing across the road toward the shelter of one of the taverns. The carriage, traveling home from Shoeburyness, had come to an abrupt halt beside the procession.

Emily, whose arms were aching with the weight of the child, did not hesitate when she heard the invitation. She had been longing to see the child safe in somebody else's arms, but so far the child had screamed and clung to her like a limpet every time she had tried to pass her over. In desperation Emily had carried her ashore and now, in desperation, she thrust her into the carriage.

"Please take her!"

"Pick her up and get in," the woman said.

"I want to go back—" Emily started. But the woman's face in the light of the carriage lamp stopped her argument. It was not the sort of face one argued with. And there were cushions in the carriage and a carpet on the floor. Emily climbed in wearily and took the little girl on her lap once more, hustling up to make room for the two soaked, garrulous old women. The carriage rocked with a motion far kinder than that of *My Alice* and Emily was able to sit back for the first time in weeks without having to think about banging her head on the deck beams. On the carpeted floor the liquid mud ran out of her split shoes. She could feel the grit under her toes. Opposite her the owner of the carriage was calling out of the window. "Drive on! Drive on!"

The carriage lurched and started to move, and Emily was glad for the darkness as they pulled away from the scurrying lanterns, for she was ashamed of her clothes and her matted hair and her chapped, raw hands like a fishwife's. A moment ago she had not cared. But the carriage with its opulent comfort had whisked her into another world. The white line of the breakers far out on the Maplins that she could see out of the window was suddenly as unreal as a picture in a book. Emily shivered and cuddled the sleeping girl on her lap. All the while carrying her over the mud she had kept thinking of the child's mother and her opal necklace "like a string of bird's eggs." The word "opal" had become ridiculously fixed to the child and now Emily could only think of her as Opal.

The carriage was climbing the hill up to the new town. The two women were telling their story, shrill and plaintive, and Emily shrunk silently and thankfully into her corner. She was curious to know where they were being taken and was surprised when, at the top of the hill, the carriage did not turn up the High Street, but went straight on along the terrace where the houses looked out over the estuary. The horses slowed down and came to a halt. The coachman came to the door and said, "Shall I take them round the back, m'm?"

"Certainly not," said his employer. "They may come in the front."

Emily tumbled out, losing her shoe in the gutter. Deftly she kicked the other off to join it, and in her bare feet felt much happier. Her weariness was giving way to excitement at the thought of going into a real house again, and seeing lights and a fire. The shrubs opposite, tossing in the wind, hid the shore and the turmoil of breaking water; it was sheltered in the street and smelled warm, of horses and laid dust. The houses opened straight onto the pavement, and the door was open, the lights shining out. Emily hitched the still sleeping Opal on her hip and followed the others in, over the cobbles and into a narrow carpeted hall. A woman, presumably a housekeeper, stood at the foot of the stairs with her eyes starting out of her head at the sorry spectacle of the three survivors dripping mud and salt water all over the floor.

"Mrs. Briggs, there has been a shipwreck. I want you to take these poor people downstairs and find dry clothes for them and something warm to drink. Then they can stay here for the night. The two women can go in the guest room, the girl in the housemaid's room, and the child on the couch in Selina's bedroom. Can you see to that?"

For the first time Emily had a good look at their deliverer. She was a tall, formidable woman of about sixty, dressed in gray. Beneath her mantle she was in evening dress, which trailed in magnificent disdain over the muddy footprints as she went up the stairs. Her face was fine drawn with a thin, sad mouth, a hooked autocratic nose, and the eyes that Emily had already decided not to argue with. She delivered her speech quite calmly, as if shipwrecks happened every day, and disappeared upstairs. The housekeeper, after opening and shutting her mouth several times, said, "Yes, Mrs. Seymour," and glared at her charges.

"If you go down the back stairs into the kitchen, I'll fetch some clothes for you," she said dourly, indicating the back stairs at the end of the hall with a nod of her head. She was an angular woman with a face like vinegar. Emily noticed her wrists, which looked capable of stopping a runaway six-horse coach without any difficulty.

After five weeks on *My Alice* the warmth and the comfort of the strictly utilitarian basement kitchen put Emily into a dreamy trance from which even the hostility of Mrs. Briggs did not arouse her. She took off her wet clothes and put on a fine embroidered shift that was passed to her and dressed Opal in a red flannel petticoat that had once, presumably, been Miss Selina's. After all she had endured for Opal's sake, she now felt quite fiercely protective toward the child, and when Mrs. Briggs moved to take the little girl up to "the couch in Selina's bedroom" Emily protested.

"Please, she will sleep with me. We can share a bed," she said. Opal, clinging to her, her bewildered blue eyes shedding noisy tears all over Emily's new finery, decided the issue. Emily, still carrying Opal, found herself climbing flights of carpeted stairs behind Mrs. Briggs's candle. There was a sloping roof and a narrow bed and, for an instant in the candlelight, a text on the wall which said: "In the hour of death and in the hour of judgment, good Lord deliver me."

Emily felt she was in paradise. The sloping roof was a hundred feet high after the smack's cramped beams. The bed smelled of clean washing. It did not rock or lie at an angle on the ebb nor shed its stinking straw at every movement. With Opal pressed close beside her, Emily slept.

"What is your name?"
"Emily Garland, ma'am."
"Where do you live?"
"Here in Southend, ma'am."
Mrs. Seymour looked closely at Emily. Emily, having decided before the interview not to complicate matters by telling untruths (after all, Mrs. Seymour, grand as she was, had no power to send her back to Bradwell) hastened to explain.

"My brother has a smack, ma'am, and we went out to the wreck and brought those people back."

"You mean you are one of the rescuers, rather than one of the rescued?" Mrs. Seymour was surprised. "Surely it was no job for a woman, going out in that storm to a wreck?"

"I happened to be on the smack when we saw the distress signals."

"You happened to be on the smack?" Mrs. Seymour looked at her inquiringly. "Don't tell me you are a sailor by profession?"

Emily, in spite of having decided to tell the truth, hesitated. It wasn't easy to admit to homelessness. It was an admission to a station in life that she had never been able to bring herself to accept, in spite of all evidence to the contrary. Only the most optimistic could call *My Alice* a home, especially when she wasn't even within sight for twelve hours out of the twenty-four.

Emily admitted that she lived on her brother's smack.

"Where do your parents live?"

"I have no parents."

"Have you no relations beside your brother?"

Emily hesitated only fractionally this time. "No," she said.

"It is a very strange life for a young girl." Mrs. Seymour observed with distaste. Silently Emily agreed.

"You have an intelligent face," Mrs. Seymour said, after a short pause. It was Emily's turn to be surprised. "I wonder if you are honest?"

Emily did not know whether the remark was a question or not, but affirmed that she was. She wasn't sure why Mrs. Seymour was questioning her, having expected to be shown out into the street before breakfast. She felt uncomfortable standing before the lady of the house in what she was sure was one of the lady's own outmoded dresses; it had an unfashionably wide skirt under which her still bare feet were mercifully hidden. She was awed by the splendor of the morning room where her interrogator was still taking her coffee from behind a small table set with silver and fine china, and did not want the elegance and comfort to spoil her for *My Alice* when she got back to the shore. She had set her mind firmly away from the little attic room with its white, clean bed the moment she had shut the door behind her. She kept thinking of Toby wondering where she had gone.

"Have you ever worked in domestic service?"

The question jolted Emily. "No—er—no, ma'am," she gasped. "But I—"

"You could learn, I dare say. I need a housemaid, but you have a very strange background. . . ." Mrs. Seymour was looking at Emily doubtfully. Emily, not knowing whether she had been offered a job or merely heard Mrs.

Seymour reflecting to no purpose, stood trembling with anticipation.

"I could take you on trial for a week perhaps. . . . Would you like to work here as a housemaid? I paid the last girl ten pounds a year, Sunday afternoons free and one day a month. Breakages to be paid for." Mrs. Seymour was obviously offering the situation against her better judgment. Her expression was reluctant. "Well?"

"Oh, yes, ma'am. Please, I should like to," Emily breathed.

"You can start straight away, and I'll see how you get on. I dismissed the last girl because she was slovenly, and the one before that because she drank. Mrs. Briggs will tell you what you have to do."

"Thank you, ma'am."

"Very well."

Emily supposed that the interview was at an end and backed nervously to the door, where she collided with a girl just coming in. The girl gave her a haughty, peevish look. She was about eighteen and Emily had an impression of a far from demure face; the eyes positively flashed. Emily begged her pardon, and as she shut the door she heard the girl say, "Is that a new maid, Mama?"

Miss Selina, Emily supposed. Her heart was thumping with excitement. The hall was filled with morning sunlight and the dark wood glowed. Emily took it as a welcome. The little white bed was hers. She could hardly believe her fortune. What would Toby say, she thought as she went back down the stairs to the kitchen. A house, a real house to live in, with high white ceilings and the smell of mutton roasting. . . .

"Well, miss?" Mrs. Briggs was looking at her sarcastically as she stood at the kitchen door. "Are you our new recruit?"

"You mean—"

"Mrs. Seymour signed you on, eh? Well, I hope you're a sight better than the last one we had, that's all. I'll get you fitted out you can start work."

Emily realized, after a quick, searching look at Mrs. Briggs, that there would be a price to pay for her white bed and high ceilings. A vinegar efficiency marked Mrs. Briggs; the sinews stood out in her neck and arms, and her lips were tight and disapproving. Everything she touched she thumped and pushed, and her starched apron crackled with zest. The kitchen was her territory and her authority was far fiercer, if less impressive, than Mrs. Seymour's in the morning room.

"A good bath is what you want," she said to Emily. "I'll just get Miss Selina's breakfast and then see to you."

The talkative old women had obviously been dispatched, but Opal sat at the table, wide-eyed, before a dish of porridge. She wasn't a pretty little thing, but freckled and button-nosed, her eyes a pale, sad blue. They brightened a little at the sight of Emily, and Emily knew they were allies. She didn't dare ask what was to happen to the child. Mrs. Briggs banged about setting things on a sliver tray and Emily looked cautiously around the kitchen, taking in her new home. It was rather dark; a large kitchen range on which several pots were simmering over the fire took up most of one wall, with tall cupboards on either side, and a large working table filled most of the floor. Beyond was a small scullery where another woman was scrubbing vegetables at the sink. She was fat and slow and had an amiable red face.

"What about breakfast for Mr. Adam?" she was saying to Mrs. Briggs. The question seemed to amuse her for she chuckled.

"No breakfast for those as don't come home to eat it," Mrs. Briggs said meaningly.

"That's twice this week," said the fat woman.

"Where does he get to? That's what I'd like to know." Mrs. Briggs had assembled a mass of delicate china and silver on her tray with no apparent damage from her heavyhandedness, and prepared to take it up to the morning room. "Open the door," she said to Emily.

She swept out and Emily said to the fat woman, "Who is Mr. Adam?" She wouldn't have dared ask Mrs. Briggs.

"Mr. Adam is the son of the house. And a real—" The woman paused, and thought better of it. "What's your name?"

"Emily."

"I'm Mrs. Noakes. Cook, you know. Live out. Where are you from?"

Emily explained about living on the smack to the astonished cook, until Mrs. Briggs came back, clapping her hands in a businesslike fashion on her starched apron.

"Well, Mrs. Noakes, if you've finished in the scullery, Emily here can get cleaned up and I'll find her some proper clothes."

She went to the cupboard and handed Emily a new bar of yellow soap and a towel as brisk as a doormat. "I'll lock the door in case Gregory comes for his tea," she said, shooting the bolts of the back door home with a crash. (Gregory, Emily learned later, was the coachman who lived in the mews at the back.) "And get your head washed. I don't want lice in my maid's room again."

With this dour advice Emily found herself alone at the stone sink, looking at her reflection in a small cracked mirror that hung over the solitary cold tap. She wasn't exactly surprised, on examining what she saw, at Mrs. Briggs's lack of respect for her appearance. Her hair was a dull bundle of frayed rope and her neck had a tide mark round it. She looked older than when she had seen herself last, her eyes fiercer and her cheekbones more prominent. She undressed to her grubby petticoat and put her head under the tap. After the drudgery of keeping the water cask full aboard *My Alice*, unlimited water out of a tap was a luxury, and to be clean all over, smelling of soap, tingling and shivering, was a further luxury. She wrapped the towel

around her and spread her hair out over it. Mrs. Briggs came in and glared at her.

"Hm," she said.

Emily, discouraged, looked at her anxiously.

"Come and get dried by the fire then. Don't stand there staring. There's work to be done."

Emily padded back into the kitchen and Mrs. Briggs combed her hair with what Emily strongly suspected was a horse comb out of the mews. Half scalped, she sat with her back to the fire while Mrs. Briggs sorted out the array of clothing she had brought downstairs with her. Mrs. Noakes was beating something in a basin at the table, and feeding Opal tidbits out of the raisin jar.

"My, you're a skinny one," Mrs. Noakes said complacently to Emily. "She won't need any stays, Mrs. Briggs."

"All girls should wear stays, thin or not," said Mrs. Briggs. "I've found her some of Miss Selina's that she finished with."

"Miss Selina pulls hers tight enough. She'll bust something one of these days. And it won't be the stays," said Mrs. Noakes. "Here, love." She popped another raisin into Opal's mouth.

Mrs. Briggs laced Emily up with the same vigor with which she had combed her hair. Emily quickly took a deep breath and resisted with her diaphragm, and found to her relief that the stays had already worn out most of their energy on Miss Selina. She could still breathe. Two starched petticoats, a gray dress with long sleeves, and a high white collar and cuffs and an apron as stiff as Mrs. Briggs's own went on top.

"That's for morning," Mrs. Briggs was saying. "You change into black in the afternoon and remember, always put a clean apron on to answer the door. There's a clean one kept specially in the hall cupboard. I'll show you in a minute. Do your hair now—nothing fancy please—and I'll tell you what's expected of you. Here are some shoes. Miss Selina threw them out last week. They're too fine for you, but I haven't anything else at the moment."

When Emily was ready, feeling very strange and rather hot, Mrs. Briggs took her on a tour of the house. The house was tall, narrow, and simply arranged, with two main rooms, one facing the front and one the back, on each floor. Downstairs there was the morning room at the front and dining room at the back; on the first floor there was Mrs. Seymour's sitting room at the front and Mr. Adam's room behind, and on the second floor were Miss Selina's room and Mrs. Seymour's bedroom at the front and back respectively. There was also a guest room and, in the attic, two small bedrooms, one Mrs. Briggs's and the other Emily's, where she had slept the night before. The whole was linked with steep staircases and narrow landings which Emily soon saw were going to give her plenty of exercise. As they toured the house Mrs. Briggs carried on a résumé of Emily's duties.

"You'll get up at five and light the kitchen fire and clean out the grates in the living rooms and dining room, then sweep and polish the downstairs rooms and Mrs. Seymour's sitting room. Do the stairs, the hall, the front doorstep, brasses, and lamp glasses. Then you light the fires and carry hot water upstairs, and come down and help me prepare breakfast. You eat yours then and afterwards wait on Mrs. Seymour. Then you can do the bedrooms and empty the slops, answer the door and deliver any messages there might be. At lunch you wait at table and wash up afterwards. Then you change and there's the ironing to do in the afternoon, or if not, there's always sewing. Serve tea at four—Mrs. Seymour's taken to this new-fangled habit of tea—and after that we get on preparing for dinner. You lay the table and wait on, then wash up and see to the bedrooms. Empty the slops and refill the ewers. In the winter there's the warming pans, but not now. . . ."

Emily, having listened but hardly digested, followed Mrs. Briggs in a daze. The front rooms, filled with sun, showed a sun-laced estuary, all light and serenity, with bawleys and schooners moving slowly down river like toys. Emily could even see *My Alice*. If only Toby knew, she thought! Somewhere in the formidable timetable Mrs. Briggs was reciting, Emily knew she must find a few minutes to see Toby. The agonies of the night before had taken on a dreamlike unreality. Emily's head reeled as she followed the housekeeper through the house. Back in the hall again, Mrs. Briggs showed her the cupboard where all the tools of her new trade were kept. The cupboard door was directly opposite the door of the morning room, and as she stood there Emily could not help but become aware of a fierce argument going on between Mrs. Seymour and her daughter. Selina's raised, almost hysterical voice, came quite clearly.

"It's always the same! Why don't you let me? Girls don't sit at home any longer! Tapestry and music and croquet!" The scorn in Selina's voice vibrated through the door. "I've got a brain! I want to use it, I want to learn something. I want to do something useful. Why can't I be a nurse? What's so disgusting about it?"

Even Mrs. Briggs could hardly ignore the tirade. She shut the broom cupboard door with a sharp crack and muttered. "Lord love us! A nurse! Whatever next?" Then she took Emily briskly by the arm and hurried her down the hall and into the kitchen.

"Miss Selina's a willful girl," she said severely to Emily. "But what goes on in the family doesn't concern us. Remember that."

Mrs. Noakes looked at Emily across the table and gave her a big wink.

"Up to her tantrums again then, Mrs. Briggs? I wonder Mrs. Seymour doesn't give her a good slap."

"The whole house could hear her, wanting to be a nurse." said Mrs. Briggs.

"Ah, that's her young man's influence, if you ask me. The medical student from Edinburgh. She's never been the same since he spent Christmas with his aunt along the terrace. Given her ideas, he has. Tch, tch, tch—" Mrs. Noakes clicked her tongue happily.

"That's enough, Mrs. Noakes," said the housekeeper sharply. "What's happened to the child?"

Emily had noticed that Opal had vanished.

"The man from the orphanage called and took her. Mrs. Seymour sent Gregory up with a message for him. Poor little mite."

"Well, that's a problem solved. Now Emily, get started on the bedrooms. I'll be up shortly to see you're doing it properly. Hurry up."

Emily, shocked by Opal's swift dispatch, did as she was told. She gathered her tools together and went upstairs. Loud sobbing was coming from Miss Selina's bedroom, so she retreated to Mr. Adam's. She was fascinated, in spite of Mrs. Briggs's warning, by what didn't concern her. Not only the willful Miss Selina, but Adam who was "a real—"

A real what? His room gave her no clues. It was somber and
austere, and rather untidy. It was more like a study than a
bedroom, for against the wall was a large desk, and the
alcove beside the fireplace was filled with books. A few
clothes were flung about, including a very muddy pair of
trousers, which rather surprised Emily. The bed was covered
with a dark green quilt and the floor with brown skin rugs.
Apart from two bottles of brandy hidden behind some
large books in the bookcase, there was no evidence of dis-
sipation or vanity or gay living at all. Emily was rather disappointed. The only object she found of interest was on
the desk: a builder's model of a small yacht. It was about
two feet long, and perfect in every detail with its sails of
fine cotton and rigging of twine. Even its name was carved
in tiny, elegant letters across the stern, and gilded: *Maplin
Bird*.

Emily looked at it for some time. A small, awful doubt
stirred somewhere in the pit of her stomach, and died.

She picked up her duster and started energetically dusting the mantel shelf.

A Call From the Customs

Toby looked at his sister in amazement.

"Emmy! Wherever have you been? And whatever—"
His eyebrows almost disappeared into the curly tangle of
unkempt hair over his forehead as Emily flung back her
old shawl and slowly turned around in front of him. She
was in her afternoon black, but without the apron.

"Aren't I elegant?" She thrust out one of Miss Selina's
dainty shoes from underneath her skirt. "Look at that."

"Well, fancy old Emmy, eh!" Toby grinned. "You've got
a job, I take it? Lady's maid or something?"

"Well, housemaid really," Emily admitted. "Up there."
She nodded her head up the hill. Mrs. Briggs had allowed
her out after dinner. She told Toby the tale of her adventures and he stood on the shore, smiling at her, and nod-
ding.

"It did us some good, then, going out to the old wreck!
We didn't know at the time."

"Listen, I must go back. Mrs. Briggs only let me out for
twenty minutes. She's the housekeeper, a real old dragon.
But it doesn't matter about her—I've got a room to myself.
It looks out over the estuary and I can see *My Alice*."

Emily chattered on as they walked slowly back up the hill to the terrace. Toby had not heard her so animated since they left home. He felt a great weight lifted off his conscience at the thought of Emily with a place to belong to, and his own future became untangled as he climbed the hill, hands in pockets. He had been going up to the "Ship" when Emily met him, to meet Dick. Now he knew he would have something to tell him.

"This straightens out a lot of things," he said to Emily. "It means I can take up Dick's offer."

"What's Dick's offer?"

"Well, you know Leigh is their home ground? They have a cottage there. I think Dick's parents quarreled and they moved out—'to teach the old woman a lesson,' Dick said. Anyway, it's patched up now and Dick's father has gone back home. Dick said I could go and live with them if I wanted. I couldn't with you, but now you are settled it might be a good idea."

He looked at Emily rather challengingly, and Emily knew straightway that he guessed she would not like the idea.

"To live with Dick's family?" Her tone was dubious.

"I wouldn't mind having a roof over my head at times, same as you," Toby said rather bitterly.

"But Dick—"

"What have you got against Dick? I'd have found it much harder making a living here without his help, I can tell you."

Emily wasn't going to tell Toby what she had against Dick, but the thought of Dick's insolent black eyes and brawling ways disturbed her. She had a strong suspicion that Dick and his family were neither honest nor respectable and, while she appreciated their offhand generosity, she did not want Toby to fall under their influence. But what could she say, with her own little room up the hill?

"Very well. You must let me know when you go. And where the cottage is. Then I can come and see you when I get a day off."

"Leigh's not far. You can walk along the beach." Toby was relieved that Emily was not turning sisterly on him, in spite of the doubt in her eyes. He smiled at her approvingly. He thought she looked very handsome in her black dress, her skin glowing white with cleanliness and her tawny hair done up tight and shining at the back of her head. He thought of her last night, taut with fear and streaming with the rain and the sea as the old smack pitched out toward the wreck.

"It'll be all right, Emmy. We're getting settled now. Who knows, we might have our own cottage in a year or two. I'm glad you found a place."

"The place found me," Emily said, thinking of the coach and Mrs. Seymour snapping at her to pick up Opal. "That little girl," she added. "The orphanage took her." She had kept thinking about Opal at intervals all through the day, with an empty feeling inside her as if, after all she had done, she had, at the end, let the child down. Emily didn't think Opal would like the orphanage. She turned to say good-bye to Toby as they reached the top of the hill, and found she had a sudden ridiculous longing to go back with him to *My Alice*. He looked so familiar standing there, so handsome and so vulnerable. To her amazement a great rush of tears came into her eyes, and she said good-bye abruptly, and hurried away down past the mews at the back to the terrace to let herself in at the kitchen door.

Mrs. Briggs was just going out.

"Good, you're back in time I see," she said, grimly approving, "Now stay in the kitchen, and don't let anyone in, whoever it may be. The family is all out, so you'll be alone in the house. Don't think you can use your time peeping and meddling now, because I shall *know*. I have my ways of knowing." Her gray eyes almost shriveled Emily, who nodded nervously. "I shall only be gone a few minutes. There are some sheets to mend there on the table, so you needn't be idle. Remember what I said."

Emily was glad when Mrs. Briggs had gone. She far preferred to be alone than to sit with Mrs. Briggs. It was nine o'clock and almost dark, but the gas lamps gave a good light for sewing. Emily had such a lot to think about that she would have preferred to just sit by the fire, without sewing, but she was frightened of Mrs. Briggs and made obedient patches, yawning over the needle. The house felt strange, empty and aloof around her; she felt cut off and forgotten. She kept thinking of Toby in the cosy noise of the "Ship," making his plans with Dick. Easygoing, easily persuaded Toby, whom her mother had worried about . . . Emily knew that, with Mrs. Briggs's timetable before her, she was going to have precious little time to keep an eye on him.

All the time Emily expected Mrs. Briggs to return, but after half an hour or so she began to suspect that the housekeeper had said she would only be a few minutes to frighten Emily out of "peeping and meddling." Once the front door slammed. Emily shot up from her sewing, catching her breath, and heard footsteps hurrying up the stairs, eager bounding footsteps not in the least suggestive of Mrs. Briggs. Nor did they sound like Mrs. Seymour's. Emily strained her ears nervously. Mrs. Briggs had said, "Don't let anyone in," but hadn't mentioned the possibility of anyone letting himself in.

"It must be Mr. Adam," Emily thought, not without curiosity. There wasn't anyone else it could be. The house was silent again, but it was an aware silence. Emily finished her sewing and sat anxiously, sorry that Mrs. Briggs had said nothing about her going to bed. She kept listening upstairs, and trying to put a face to Mr. Adam. How old was he? Was he handsome? What did he do? What was he doing in his bleak, masculine room with the books and the brandy and the *Maplin Bird*?

A loud knock at the front door made her leap out of her chair. She felt her heart pounding with apprehension. The clock showed past ten o'clock—surely too late for anyone respectable to be calling. And Mrs. Briggs's advice was still firm in Emily's mind. But perhaps it *was* Mrs. Briggs? After her first fright at the sudden noise, Emily calmed down, realizing how stupid she was being. It was her job to answer the door, after all. Whoever it was upstairs wasn't worrying.

She went down the hall, pulled back the bolt, and opened the door very cautiously. Two men stood there. The light shone on their faces. Emily stared.

"Mr. Adam Seymour?" one inquired. "We'd like a few words with him please."

The man who spoke was a policeman. The man with him was a customs man. He wore no uniform, but Emily, true smackman's daughter, knew he was a customs man. Toby had pointed him out a week or two earlier. She thought quickly, instinctively "against" the two men that stood on the doorstep. She had not yet met Adam Seymour,

but she was sure he didn't want to see these particular visitors.

"There's nobody in but me," she said.

"We have good reason to believe that Mr. Seymour is at home," the policeman said.

"I didn't hear anyone come in, but I'll go and see," Emily said steadily.

"Very well."

She left the door on the chain so that the men couldn't enter and hurried up the stairs. She was excited and nervous at once, and knocked rapidly on Adam's door. It opened almost immediately.

"Who is it?" the man said, swiftly and quietly.

"A policeman and a customs man, sir, asking for you."

She looked up to see the reaction, and saw alarm curiously mingled with amusement in a pair of very lively blue eyes.

"I'm not in then," he said. "What did you tell them?"

"I told them that, sir, but said I'd to look to make sure."

"Well, you've made sure, haven't you? I'm not in. Good girl. Let me know when you've got rid of them." He paused, then added, "Are the family all out?"

"Yes, sir."

"Thank God for that."

Emily went back downstairs to the front door. She did not remove the chain, but spoke through the gap.

"No, he's not in."

The two men looked at each other, and she knew they didn't believe her. The customs man said, "I'd like to look for myself."

"I've orders to let nobody in," Emily said.

At least, she thought, they weren't thin enough to get through the gap. But she was frightened of the power of the law. The customs man looked angry, but the policeman said something to him in a low voice that Emily did not catch. They turned away and the policeman gave her an abrupt good night. Emily shut the door and leaned against it, gathering her wits. She heard the heavy boots walking away, and then silence again. The gas lamp hissed. She felt rather shaken.

"Have they gone?" Adam was looking over the banisters.

"Yes, sir."

"What did they say?"

Adam came downstairs, staring at her curiously. Emily gave him an account of the interview, wishing she knew what his crime was. He did not seem to be very worried; she got the impression that he was more frightened of his mother than of the police.

"They timed their call well. Don't say a word of this to anyone," he instructed. "I think I shall have to go, but I'm blowed if I'm going to miss a night's sleep first."

He yawned. He looked tired, Emily decided, with shadows under his eyes. His skin was brown from the weather; he had the same eyes as Selina but his hair was black and slightly curling and he had let it grow down over his cheekbones to form a very becoming set of whiskers. He gave Emily the impression of restlessness and impatience; there was none of Mrs. Seymour's serenity about him. He was in his middle twenties, she guessed, lithe and quick in his movements.

He turned to go back upstairs, but paused on the second step and looked at Emily again.

"You were very sensible just now. I haven't seen you before, have I? Are you new?"

"Yes, sir."

"What's your name?"

"Emily, sir."

"Rather you than Mrs. Briggs," he said. He climbed three more stairs, then thought of something else. "If my mother wants to know where I am in the morning, tell her I've ridden out to Wakering to see about the delivery of the bricks. She'll like that."

He grinned.

"Yes, sir."

He disappeared upstairs. Emily went back to the kitchen,

mystified and worried. Her curiosity about Adam had been increased rather than satisfied by her unexpected meeting and she was beginning to think that her new acquaintances were hardly more respectable than her old ones on the shore.

"For all their grandeur," she thought, remembering Selina's unladylike outburst by the broom cupboard.

She was so tired now after her disturbed evening and the day's excitements—not to mention the chores—that she

was almost asleep when Mrs. Briggs came in. She was ordered to bed, and fell asleep before she had a chance to wonder any more. Then in no time, it seemed, she was at work again, cleaning, beating, and polishing downstairs and later carrying up steaming jugs of water to the bedrooms. Selina was under the bedclothes and Emily's presence was acknowledged by a sleepy grunt. Emily, wondering how anyone could make a room so untidy in a mere twelve hours or so, opened the curtains and retreated.

Picking up the second jug, she knocked on Adam's door. There was no reply. She knocked again, then, as there was still no answer, she opened the door and went in. The room was empty and bare. The curtains were drawn back, and one of the long windows that led out on to an iron balcony at the back of the house was open. From the balcony, steps led down into the back garden.

"How useful for Adam," Emily thought.

There was nothing to show that he had ever come home, only—strangely—a fire burning in the grate. Something in the ashes caught Emily's eye. She crossed to the fireplace and saw that the fuel was wood: it was the model of the little yacht, the *Maplin Bird*. Only the bowsprit, hanging out of the grate on the last unburned cotton shroud, was still recognizable. Emily stooped and pushed it into the embers. It flared up, and the boat was gone.

Emily's Secret

It took Emily several weeks to feel she knew the occupants of the Seymour house and to understand Mrs. Noakes's winks and innuendoes, to find out why the police were interested in Mr. Adam, why Miss Selina was discontented and what Mrs. Seymour's interests were. After her first day's trip down to the shore to see Toby, Emily did not go outside again, save to hang out the washing. The ever-changing panorama of the shore and the estuary out of the tall front windows was more like an intricate mural than reality; the smell of seaweed had been exchanged for that of wax polish and soap. Emily knew she had gotten her heart's desire, but it was at a price.

"Oh, you sea!" she whispered, leaning out of her window in the roof to cool her face. The woods of Kent were gold in the evening sun, far away across a golden haze of calm water. The tide roamed with a breadth that Emily envied; she felt like a trapped animal in the house. She had paid for her security with physical freedom and sometimes, as at this moment, she felt it was like paying with her soul.

"Idiot!" she said to herself. "What do you want? Why do you complain? You have everything you want."

But all her life, till now, she had been free to wander along the sea walls and the strips of shingle; it had been as natural to her as breathing, the sky and the smell of the Essex mud. The smell of dust and polish choked her when outside the windows the sun was shimmering across the wet mud flats. Officially she was free on Sunday afternoon but unofficially she discovered she was expected to go to church. The church smelled of dust and polish. Emily prayed for the sun and the grass.

Her own room was very small, but she loved it. With its view out over the estuary, it was, at least, as near to the fresh air as she was likely to get, and she had her own bits and pieces there, her picture of the geese flying over the marshes and the photo of her mother and father. Besides the bed, she had a chest of drawers and a chair, their varnish rather scratched and battered. The sloping roof and walls were covered with a faded wallpaper of tortuous roses with writhing leaves and stems, the floor was stained and sparely covered with an old brown rug. She spent little enough time in it, but it was pleasant to know there was somewhere, and that she didn't have to share a room with Mrs. Briggs. Mrs. Briggs was humorless and tart. Emily didn't like her, although she had to admit that she was fair. In spite of her title, Emily didn't think she had ever been married, not like Mrs. Noakes with her twelve children and shrimping husband.

Mrs. Seymour was a widow, and the owner of a good deal of property in the district. She had put some of her money into the new building that was going on in Southend, and Adam was supposed to be her business manager, in charge of the negotiations and supplies. Just how efficient he was at the job Emily could only guess, but Mrs. Noakes didn't have a very high opinion of his abilities.

"I wouldn't trust him with my fortune, and that's for sure," she told Emily. "Too fond of gallivanting around the countryside, not to mention the brandy bottle. He misses a father, that's his trouble."

Adam had stayed away two days after the visit from the police. They did not call again, and only Emily knew of the first visit. When he came back, Adam asked Emily if his mother had found out. He did not treat her like the maid, but spoke to her as an equal, almost as an accomplice. He had an easy charm with him, and none of the patronage or stilted formality of the young men that occasionally came to dinner with Mrs. Seymour and Selina. Adam used to moan about the dinners but his mother was adept at seeing he did not avoid his social duties. "Make sure you remind Adam, and put his clothes out for him," she would order Mrs. Briggs. Adam would groan again and stamp about his room, and Emily, when she served at table, saw his boredom and indifference. When he did not choose to be charming he could be insufferable, she realized. Whatever his interests, they were not at home.

"He'll wear the legs off that mare of his," Old Gregory grumbled when he came into the kitchen for a drink in the morning. "Always galloping off to heaven knows where. Come back two days later and hand her over, caked in sweat. What's it got to do with building houses, I'd like to know?"

Often Adam would be away at night or, sometimes, when Emily went up to do the bedrooms, she would find him sprawled asleep at ten in the morning. Nobody mentioned the *Maplin Bird,* and Emily began to wonder if there had ever been such a craft. If Mrs. Seymour disapproved of her son, she made no sign. She did not scold him as she did Selina, but Emily had a feeling that the dour pity in her eyes was for Adam. Emily did not think it would be very comfortable to have Mrs. Seymour for a mother. Mrs. Seymour was old-fashioned in her outlook, very formal and shrewd. It was hard to tell what she was thinking behind the austere façade, but Emily guessed that the eyes missed very little. Although she never entered the kitchen, she knew everything that went on there, and Emily had a suspicion that she perhaps knew more about Adam and his discussed absences than he would have liked. She was a forbidding figure with her gray eyes, her iron-gray hair dressed elaborately at the back of her head, and dark, severe dresses. She had few friends and had apparently been widowed for several years; the spirit of Mr. Seymour did not seem to weigh heavily upon her and Emily pictured him as a quiet, overwhelmed man whose weaknesses were now materializing in the unsatisfactory son. And the unsatisfactory daughter.

"Little baggage!" Mrs. Noakes said scornfully. "Everything in the world she's got, and she's never content. Always wanting the moon."

The moon was, for Selina, the chance of going out to work. "First, she wanted to be a teacher," Mrs. Noakes told Emily. "Now it seems it's nursing, since she's met that young doctor fellow. Tomorrow it'll be something else. Just because a few women in London are making themselves ridiculous trying to get into the university, young madam thinks she'd like to do the same! She's always talking about going to study in London—of all the ideas! A girl in her position wanting to work! Some people don't know when they're well off. Change places with us who *have* to work for a week or so, and she'd soon change her mind."

Emily agreed that it was rather odd of Selina. She seemed to have a very comfortable life as far as Emily could make out, often getting up nearer lunch time than breakfast time, and sitting around for the rest of the day doing embroidery or playing the piano. Occasionally she went visting with her mother, and in the evenings they might go out to dinner. Selina had a wardrobe full of fine clothes and evening dresses that made Emily's eyes boggle, yet she gave no indication of enjoying them. She was rude to the servants, subdued with her mother—apart from the occasional outbursts —and Emily thought that she was really unhappy: her eyes were bored and her lips sulky. She was a handsome girl, apart from her discontent, tall and well-built ("plump," said Mrs. Noakes plainly) with dark, curling hair and a regal, imposing carriage. Emily privately thought her rather impressive, but did not see that she had anything to complain about.

"It's strange," Emily thought to herself, "how we all complain." She herself had everything she wanted, yet there were times when her misery was almost a physical pain. Her work was arduous and boring, but her own private miseries were not concerned with work; they were caused by what she could only suppose was homesickness, a perverse longing for all those things she had been most anxious to be rid of when she had them: the old cottage at Bradwell and the stinking cuddy of *My Alice,* as well as the sea wall air and—most of all—Toby. Once, after she had been turning out the bedrooms, Mrs. Briggs said to her when she came back to the kitchen, "Oh, someone called for you. Said he was your brother. I told him we don't see our relations here until we're off duty and he could call back after dinner. He left a message." Emily was speechless at Mrs. Briggs's inhumanity; it was beyond her comprehension. When she laid the lunch she could see *My Alice* getting up sail off the pier end. The sight of the old smack disappearing out across the estuary made her bite her lip to stop the tears coming. Boats could not "call back after dinner," as Mrs. Briggs seemed to think. The message was brief. It just said, "End cottage by the cockle shed. Leigh. Love Toby."

She did not see Toby again for a month, and that was on a Sunday when she had a whole day to herself—her first since she started work. She hardly slept the night before with excitement at the thought of her freedom, and soon after breakfast was running like a goat down the slithering sandy cliffs to the shoreline, laughing out loud at the feel of the damp air on her face. She had her own old muslin dress on and her hair was already falling loose with her leaping. She had not run for weeks. The tide was high and the young trees dipped almost to the water in places and there were branches in the shingle, tangled with seaweed and old fishing nets, and driftwood white as bone and an old shoe. It was all untidy and wild and unpolished. Emily kicked the shingle and felt the grit in her shoes again. The shore was her own.

Ahead of her the bare nose of Canvey Island curved out, and the silver tongue of Leigh gut ran in, with the bawleys at anchor and a church bell pealing lazily. It was warm and there were skylarks along the cliffs and the little white bellies of the sandpipers along the water line. Soon she could see the foreshore of the old port, the weatherboard cottages higgledy-piggledy along the waterfront and the old church sticking up on the hill. The thought of Toby

started her running again, and she went up into the village
and searched the waterfront until she found him sitting on
the sea wall with Dick, splicing a frayed halyard. They
were laughing at something and did not see her immediately. Emily had a good look at Toby sitting there carelessly,
as disheveled and dirty-looking as she had ever seen him,
his buttonless shirt showing a brown, broad chest, his feet
bare, his hair tangled over his forehead, and she knew that
even in a month he had changed, grown up, hardened.
She felt lost for a moment, as if he were a stranger, but
then he saw her and his face lit up. He dropped his work
and leaped off the sea wall with a shout.

"Emmy! Why, Emmy! Has the old trout let you off for the day then? Emmy, how good to see you! Can you stay for a bit?"

Work was abandoned and the three of them went roaming the shore, throwing stones at the gulls, leaping the pools, and running through the sun-shimmering mud and sand and up through the fields above the shore as if they none of them knew what it was to do anything but play. It was hot and the grass was flowering, the paths were all dust and the elms heavy-headed, green topsails against the estuary sky. Emily felt drunk with the pleasure of mere freedom. Toby, if he had changed, could still throw off six years; the boys were like animals, running and wrestling in the grass, climbing trees and leaping down into the ditches. When they were tired they lay in the sun and talked, and Emily learned how *My Alice* was slowly being improved and how Toby reckoned he would be able to swap her for a bawley when she was sound, and Toby learned how many stairs there were in the terrace houses, and what an interminable lot of hot water had to be lugged up to the bedrooms. Dick lay on his back and blew grasses through his fingers. Emily supposed he was all right.

Later, when they were going back to Dick's cottage, Emily said "Have you ever heard of a boat called the *Maplin Bird?*"

She had said nothing about Adam's eccentricities and the visit of the police. Even this single question came doubtfully.

"The *Maplin Bird?* Why, yes, of course. She's the one the customs are after for running brandy in from France," Dick said carelessly.

"You know her?" Emily said.

"Know *of* her," Toby said. "Nobody exactly sees her, save way in the distance. They say she can outsail any of the revenue cutters. That's why they can't catch her."

"Who does she belong to?"

"Nobody knows," Toby said.

"But they must know."

"Well, nobody in Leigh knows. But they all reckon it's someone around here, or Paglesham way perhaps."

Emily knew, but she said nothing.

"She's not just a fishing smack," Dick said. "She pretends to be a yacht, but no one sails around here much for pleasure. She's a smuggler on a big scale, and it must pay her to take the risks she does. But she'll be caught pretty soon."

"Yes. The customs men know everyone's laughing at 'em for letting her slip through their fingers. It riles them."

"Whoever it is ought to lie low for a bit," Emily said.

"Yes, of course," Dick said. "But they're all the same, these fellows who think the risk's worth taking. They get away with it a few times, and make a load of cash, and the thing grows on them. There's plenty does it in a small way, mind you, but once or twice, just when the opportunity comes up—that's nothing. But the big ones, they always get caught because they don't know when to stop."

"I thought smuggling was finished now? Compared to how it used to be," Emily said doubtfully.

"It's not like it was say fifty—twenty—years ago," Dick said. "But there'll always be smuggling. It's natural."

"It's human nature," Toby agreed.

"You get 'em, now and again, like the *Maplin Bird,* and there's a fuss and bother and everyone talks about it, and then he's caught and that's an end to it. But all the time there's little bits of things coming and going, tobacco and wine and such like. Who's to know?"

"They're not God, the customs," Toby said. "They can't see everything."

"It'll be the same in another hundred years too," Dick said, "as long as there's things cheaper over there."

Emily walked slowly home, tired and astonished. She knew what Adam's business was now. The knowledge awed her. She wondered why she hadn't told Toby and Dick about him, and then she realized that the secret was too big to share, and that the instinct to say nothing had been the right one. It could not be lightly divulged. It was an enormous secret. And hers alone. Nobody else knew; even the customs officers didn't know all she knew, else they would have come again for Adam. They suspected, perhaps, but they didn't know about the ashes in his grate that had been the *Maplin Bird*. She didn't think even Mrs. Seymour *knew* what he was doing, even if she had her suspicions.

"But I know," said Emily to herself. She knew too, from what Dick had said, with all the natural intuition and experience of one grounded in all the many facets of local seagoing, that Adam was heading for disaster.

"He should be furtive and secret and hide away and wait," she thought. "But he's not a furtive sort of person. He enjoys it too much and they'll catch him."

She thought he must do it for the excitement rather than the money. It fitted in with what she knew of his nature, his restlessness and lack of social decorum. She tried to tell herself that he was wicked, but Adam the smuggler had a fascination that Adam the builder lacked. She was ashamed of the fact, but it was so.

It was as if, because she had been thinking about him so hard, he had received some telepathic summons, for when she climbed back up the sandy cliffs she met Adam riding home along the road from Leigh. She did not realize who it was until the horse was almost on top of her and she had stepped aside into the long grass. Then, when she glanced up and recognized the rider, she was so overcome with confusion at what she knew about him that she could scarcely reply to his greeting. Immediately she became aware of her tangled hair, her mud-splashed dress, and the sweaty glow that burned in her cheeks. She expected him to pass by, but to her surprise he reined the mare in to a walk beside her.

"I've always thought they worked you too hard," he said. "I'm glad to see you're let out occasionally."

"I—I've been to see my brother, sir," Emily said with what dignity she could muster. She didn't tell him they ran through the fields and threw stones and climbed trees all afternoon. She wanted him to think they had sat in a cool parlor and discussed politics.

"Is it true," Adam asked, "that your brother has a boat? He's a fisherman?"

In view of the day's revelations, Emily looked at Adam, startled out of her embarrassment. There did not seem to be anything but polite interest behind his question. He was smiling at her in what she thought of as "his equal way," as if she was not the housemaid, and which excused, in her eyes, any of his other grave defects. He rode with an easy, elegant confidence, but his restlessness was in the mare, who walked curvetting and chinking her bit. Her neck was covered in lather. Adam moved her off the path so that Emily could use the trodden-down way.

Emily said, "Yes, sir," cautiously.

"He lives at Leigh?"

"Yes, sir."

"What's he got? A bawley?"

"It's a smack called *My Alice*."

Emily longed to tell Adam what Dick had said about the

big ones not knowing when to stop, but dared not. Adam said, "Oh, yes, I've seen her. Registered at Maldon."

"Yes." Emily looked sideways up at Adam again. He was looking between his mare's ears, thoughtful but unworried. The sun was behind him; he looked, to Emily, far too incautious and carefree, sitting easily on the mare with the reins in one hand and a white marguerite twiddling idly in the other. His collar was open and his cravat undone; his black coat was faded but his boots shone like the mare's own damp sides. Emily could not bear that he should be so reckless.

It was growing cooler now and the estuary was smooth and dull gold below them. Behind, Leigh church was black against the sun and the cottage chimneys were making a sea mist up from the water line. Leigh gut lay like a gold thread dropped on the darkening mud. Emily wanted to tell Adam what Dick had said, but she knew it was impossible and it was as if the sun had gone in because she could not warn him. But then she thought, "He must know what he's doing. It doesn't need Dick to tell him that he will be caught. What does it matter?" That was the truth, but a great uneasiness filled Emily. She felt utterly despondent as they neared the terrace and Adam said, "Old Gregory will be glad I met you. The mare's cooled down and I can take her in without a conscience."

He smiled at her again, his charming equal smile, and swung the horse around and trotted her down the lane to the mews behind the terrace. Emily went in down the area steps, and as the kitchen door closed behind her she pretended that she knew what Adam would feel like when he went to prison.

A Meeting at Crowstone

Selina lay in bed looking at the patterns of the sun creeping through the gap in the curtains to play on the ceiling. In a moment, she knew, the maid would come in and whisk them apart, and another dreary day would begin: to dress, to take breakfast, practice the piano, a little sewing, lunch, a visit to the rectory garden party where the curate was the only unattached male between two or three dozen unattached ladies, a round of croquet, and home to a dull dinner and a duller evening. No wonder, she thought, Adam stayed at home less and less, and in consequence worried his mother more and more. If Adam suffered a quarter of the restrictions she did, Selina thought, he would have left home for good long ago.

Selina longed to leave home. She was so insufferably bored that sometimes she thought she would go mad. She wanted to go to London and do something other than embroidery—anything would do, anything to occupy her stultifying mind. Her mother resisted every suggestion; her invariable argument was that work for a girl in Selina's situation was unseemly. "But I don't want to scrub floors," Selina thought angrily. "It's not unseemly to study, to teach or nurse." Nursing was respectable since Miss Nightingale had made it so. It wasn't as if she wanted to go on the stage.

The newspapers that she wasn't supposed to read were full of reports about the forward young ladies who were trying to get into colleges to take degrees along with the men, and when Selina saw her mother stuffing sheets of newspaper on the fire, her lips pursed tight, she knew that the hussies had struck another blow, and she longed to be one of them. Her mother was old-fashioned and Selina considered herself as a small oasis of radical thought in the desert of provincial Southend. This, however, did not make her want to get up any earlier. She could think her radical thoughts as easily in bed as anywhere else.

A discreet knock on the door was followed by the appearance of Emily with the hot water. Selina pretended to be asleep but she watched Emily curiously. For a servant Emily had a peculiarly intelligent look about her which worried Selina. She was common enough—her brother was a fisherman, Selina had heard—but her fierce eyes and firm chin were strikingly uncommon; she would not have looked out of place at the vicarage party, Selina thought. She had none of the usual servant's scuffle and sniffs.

"*She* works hard enough," Selina thought. "I wonder if *she* thinks it's unseemly?"

Selina wished she could talk to her as if she wasn't a servant, and ask her what she thought of it all, of her mother, and Adam's gallivanting, and herself lying in bed till ten o'clock, and ask her what they talked about in the kitchen and whether she ever felt as if she didn't care whether she lived or died. But Emily, switching back the curtains, only said, "Good morning, Miss," and went out.

"Lazy slut," Emily thought. She went down to the next floor and paused on the landing to look out of the window.

She was thinking about Adam who was lying in bed with a bruise on his forehead the color of a thunder cloud and a look in his eyes to match. Nobody had heard him come in the night before. When Emily had gone to his room ten minutes earlier she had found his clothes lying in a heap on the floor dripping wet and Adam had roused himself sufficiently to tell her to take them down to the kitchen and get them dried. As it hadn't rained for the last three weeks Emily wondered what had caused him to take what must have been an involuntary swim: the clothes, the bruise, and his strange preoccupation suggested that some crisis had occurred in his life. Emily didn't think it was anything to do with the building business either. She was worried and curious. She stared absently out of the window, and as she did so she caught sight of a revenue cutter sailing slowly upriver off the end of the pier.

"Perhaps you're the cause of the trouble," she thought, her eyes on its rakish lines. The cutter was not alone. She was sailing in company, and the boat that followed her was a little black yacht with dark sails. The sweet sheer of the fast, narrow hull stirred Emily's memory. She came out of her trance and stared.

A voice behind her said suddenly, "What are you looking at?"

Emily nearly jumped out of her skin. She turned around, scarlet. Adam was standing there in his dressing gown. His eyes were on the black yacht, his lips pursed thoughtfully.

"Nothing, sir," Emily said, recovering herself. She turned to go downstairs but Adam was in her way and made no move to let her go. Emily was forced to stay where she was.

"Do you know what the *Maplin Bird* is?" Adam asked suddenly.

Emily blinked and nodded. "Isn't—isn't that the *Maplin Bird,* sir?" she murmured, her eyes going to the window.

Adam gave her a grim smile. "So you do know? I wondered. I didn't think you'd missed much—you've got too much sense. What did your brother tell you about her, eh?"

"He said she was bound to be caught, because they always are."

"He was right, then, wasn't he?"

"Yes, sir."

"And what did you tell him?"

"I told him nothing, sir."

"Good for you." Adam smiled less grimly. "Is your brother a discreet man?" he asked.

"I think so."

"I would like to meet him. Could you arrange that?"

Emily hesitated. She didn't want Toby to meet Adam. Toby had enough on his hands without getting involved with Adam's dishonesty. Adam guessed her thoughts, for he said, "I shan't get him into trouble, if that's what you're thinking."

"What—what do you want him for then?"

"Professional advice, to do with my boat," Adam nodded to the disappearing *Maplin Bird*. "Don't you trust me then?" he added as she hesitated. Emily didn't, but could hardly say so. Adam stepped forward and said quietly and earnestly, "Look, they may have my *Bird,* but they don't have me, nor either of my crew. Nor will they get us now. They didn't see us last night, for all that they took us by surprise, and now we're away there are no clues on the boat to say whose she is. The only people who know she's mine will put their hands on their hearts and swear they've never seen the owner, because she has done them proud in the past and they won't forget it. I'm as safe now as if that had never happened." He gestured out of the window to the cutter escorting his yacht.

"But why did the customs call for you that night?" Emily asked. "They must have their suspicions about something."

"Yes, they called about a packet of tobacco I was fool enough to drop out of my pocket under a tavern counter.

The customs officer was drinking there, a couple of feet from my nose. If he hadn't followed me I'd have wondered why. But they can scarcely serve me a summons on the strength of one packet of tobacco."

Emily wasn't sure if her imagination was playing her tricks, but Adam looked to her a lot less charming than usual. For the first time she found she could reconcile this Adam with the one her brain had been telling her all along existed: the ruthless and dishonest "freetrader." To be as successful as he was reputed to be, he couldn't be charming all the time. She saw now that his face was angry and hard; in the fineness of his lips she now saw cruelty, and in his eyes the gleam of fanaticism. Or was it her imagination? He was smiling again.

"You're fond of your brother, aren't you?"

"Yes. He's all I have. I don't want him to get into trouble."

"Don't worry," Adam said. "I won't hurt him." He paused. "Emily, don't say anything about this. Not downstairs, or outside, or anywhere. You realize what it means, don't you?"

"Yes, sir."

"Not a word?"

"No, sir." She wanted to add, "If you'll leave Toby alone." Adam moved to let her go by, and she found that she was almost trembling. She rushed downstairs, longing to hear Mrs. Briggs's scolding voice bringing her back to everyday things, to the slop basins and the coal buckets, so that she could forget the extraordinary things she had found out through no fault of her own.

Several days later, Toby received a message. It read:

"Dear Sir, I am a friend of your sister's and wish to ask you a favor. Perhaps you would be good enough to meet me on the beach at Crowstone 9 P.M. on Thursday?"

There was no signature. Toby, puzzled, showed it to Dick, who roared with laughter and said, "Cor, strike me! He's going to ask for your sister's hand! The sly minx! She didn't say anything about it the other Sunday."

"Oh, rubbish! She'd have told me," Toby said uneasily.

"Might be a girl," Dick teased. "It doesn't say. Emmy's told her how handsome you are and she wants a kiss."

Toby's uneasiness changed to alarm.

"What a lark!" Dick said. "Take me along, will yer?"

"No I won't," Toby said. "You don't really think it's a girl, surely? Doesn't look like a girl's writing."

"It's toff's writing."

"It doesn't smell of scent or anything."

"Go and see, blockhead. It's only tomorrow. Wash yer face, just in case."

Toby wouldn't have bothered to go, save for the mention of his sister, but, on Thursday night when the others went out to "The Peter Boat" he duly washed his face and combed his hair and set out along the beach. The tide was making; *My Alice* lay far out on the mud at the edge of the gut. Beyond her, in deep water at the mouth of the gut, guarded by the revenue cutter, was the shapely black yacht that the customs had been chasing for the last six months. Her name, the *Maplin Bird,* was carved and gilded unashamedly across her stern, and her appearance had caused quite a stir in the town. Much talked of, the *Bird* had never been seen at close quarters before. The great joke was, of course, that the *Bird* appeared to have no master, and the customs officers were not a great deal better off for having the boat. Nothing had been found aboard her, not even as much as a secret panel. She was innocent as a child. The officer aboard the cutter was chewing his handsome whiskers in vexation and the whole of Leigh was laughing at him. Toby smiled to himself with satisfaction. Nobody was ever on the side of the customs officers.

The beach was deserted as far as he could see. Toby walked on anxiously. He kept thinking that the letter was probably a hoax. If it was a girl he would cut and run for his life. If it was a toff, he would be wishing he had a best suit to put on. His work clothes were almost threadbare, but they were all he had.

"Well, this is Crowstone," he thought presently, "and I'll swear it's nine o'clock."

He looked around hesitantly. The mud glittered with a sunset light, red as copper. Beyond Canvey the sun had disappeared in a gray bank of cloud and the narrowing sea ran black between the marshes. Toby wished he were in "The Peter Boat" with Dick.

Suddenly he saw a movement in the trees on the cliffs, and a man slithered down the sandy bank onto the beach and walked toward·him. He was inconspicuously dressed in riding clothes, bare-headed, quite young, and slightly worried looking. At close quarters he was definitely a toff. If this was Emily's friend, Toby thought, she was doing well for herself. He walked to meet him.

"You're Toby Garland?"

The man held out his hand, and looked at Toby closely as he shook it. Toby nodded.

"Yes, sir."

"Emily has told me about you," the man said. "I want someone to do a job for me, a very well-paid and perfectly simple job, and I thought, if you have half the sense your sister has, you would be the man for me. Do you want a job?"

"Depends what it is," Toby said slowly. "If it's perfectly simple why is it so well paid?"

The man smiled. "Ah, the family likeness reveals itself." The smile vanished as quickly as it came. "I will tell you who I am. The name doesn't matter—if you know it, it will suit you well to forget it—but it's enough, I think, to say that I'm the owner of the *Maplin Bird*."

Toby's eyes opened very wide. He looked at Adam in astonishment, then out across the mud to the black yacht swinging to her anchor.

"You're—"

"I don't go around telling everyone this, you understand? I trust you, because Emily said I could. She didn't say you would help me, but if I tell you what I want you to do, you can make up your own mind about whether you will or not."

Toby was thinking hard, trying to work out Emily's connection with the freetrader. She had asked about the *Maplin Bird* when they had last met, but said nothing about knowing the man himself.

"What is it?" he asked cautiously.

"I want the *Bird* sailed out, at night, and taken down the estuary."

"What, from under the cutter's nose?" Toby was startled, and forgot about Emily.

"Yes. It's the last thing they'll be expecting, which is a good reason for the trick succeeding. She only needs a head start to show them a clean pair of heels. I'd do it myself, but I cannot risk getting caught now."

"What if I'm caught?" Toby thought to himself. Adam answered the unspoken question. "If you're caught, anyone in Leigh will vouch for you. A man paid you to do it, you can say. You don't know who. You didn't ask any questions. He gave you twenty-five pounds and promised you the same when you handed the boat over. Who would refuse? There'll be no danger in it for you."

"And if I was to do it, and get away, what do I do then?"

"You sail her as far as the Barrow, and on the south side you'll see the lights of a bawley. You flash her a signal and go alongside and a crew will be waiting for the *Bird*. You can transfer to the bawley and land where you will. They'll pay you the rest of your money. The *Bird* will be out of the estuary well before dawn, all being well."

"The tide turns around midnight," Toby said. "She'd need to go at high water. Drift off if the anchor warp were cut. . . ."

"And get up sail when you're clear. They might never see you go."

There was a gleam in Adam's eye. Toby stopped short suddenly. "I haven't said I'll do it," he said. "It needs thinking about."

"There isn't time to think," Adam said. "They're taking her up the river tomorrow."

"You mean—"

"Tonight. Or not at all. It's as simple as that."

Toby stood looking out across the mud, to where the *Maplin Bird* lay. There was a tight feeling in his throat. He couldn't afford to get into trouble, not this man's sort of trouble, but fifty pounds. . . . Fifty pounds was enough to set him up for life. And the plan was audacious enough to succeed.

"What if there's a guard on the yacht?"

"I'm trusting there isn't. If you row out to her and there's someone sitting up there on deck, you just say good night and row back home. There'll be no harm done. But if she's unguarded a child could do it. Look how she's lying there. Downriver of the cutter, nicely clear. Cut her warp and the tide'll take her away before they know what's happening."

Toby sensed Adam's urgency and his restraint; he respected his boldness and the devilish simplicity of his plan. He also respected the reason that stopped him from carrying it out himself. There was a considerable chance of getting caught—if he were seen going aboard, or if he failed to set the sails quickly enough. Adam could not afford to be caught now. Toby could—for fifty pounds.

"Will you do it?"

Toby nodded. "I'll try."

Adam's face lit up. "Splendid! Now listen. . . ." With a sketch in the sand he showed Toby where the bawley would be waiting. They worked out what time the two boats would meet, according to the wind and tide, and Adam gave Toby his twenty-five pounds.

"High water is eleven-twenty," Adam said, glancing at a gold watch at his waist. "Go at twelve, and they'll be waiting for you down the river. I'll go to Shoebury now and tell them to put off." He paused, and his excitement changed suddenly to caution. "Whatever happens," he said, "say nothing. If anyone wants to know anything, you don't know who I am, it was too dark for you to see me properly, you know nothing. You understand?"

"Yes. I understand."

Toby had the twenty-five pounds in his back pocket, where it was warming his seat with a comforting glow. He was

wildly happy and excited and eager to go. Adam left him, and presently Toby heard the hasty thrum of hoofs galloping along the cliff top toward Shoebury. Toby had two hours to wait and was as restless as a crab on the mud, not wanting his courage to fail him, not wanting to meet anyone, hardly wanting to think about what he had to do. It would be fatal to go back and meet Dick. He must stay hidden until the tide was high, then go out on the first of the ebb in his dinghy. Then it struck him that he could as well wait for high water aboard *My Alice* as hang around conspicuously on the beach, so he started to walk back, trying not to hurry, watching the water creep up the mud toward him, black now and unfriendly. Lights were shining on the water, the twinkling lace of lights across the river that showed the mouth of the Medway, and the nearby riding lights of the revenue cutter and the *Maplin Bird*. It was cool, with a steady blessed wind blowing down the river, but Toby could feel sweat prickling his skin. He kept thinking that to go away in the *Maplin Bird* would be like the night they went away in *My Alice,* but he had to admit that he was more afraid of the revenue officers than he was of Uncle Gideon.

Dick was still in "The Peter Boat" and there was no one on the foreshore to see him take his boat and start the long scull out to the smack. Some bawleys were coming in close-hauled down the gut, their chimneys smoking as their day's catch of shrimps was cooked aboard, and Toby, noticing their trim gear, thought of the difference twenty-five pounds was going to make to *My Alice.*

"You'll be a *Maplin Bird* by the time I've finished with you, you old wreck," he muttered to the seamy decks as he went aboard.

Then he lay on his forehatch and tried to make out what was happening aboard the revenue cutter and its prisoner which lay a mere hundred yards downriver. It was too dark to see much, but both boats seemed quiet enough; there were lights shining out of the hatches of the cutter, but, apart from the riding light, the *Maplin Bird* was in darkness. Toby took out his knife and sharpened its blade thoughtfully. Then he took the twenty-five pounds out of his back pocket and hid it in one of the old mattresses. Then he waited for the tide to turn, watching the lights and feeling the wind, and conscious of a strange tingling in his nerves. He had never dreamed he would ever stand at the tiller of the *Maplin Bird*.

The tide grew full, and was slack. *My Alice* moved slowly around her anchor and at last fell back on the ebb and the warp took up taut. Toby waited, dry-mouthed. The *Maplin Bird* had turned, and her bow pointed up the river. The revenue cutter was silent, her lights still shining, her skiff alongside. Toby had not heard nor seen any movement on her for the last hour. He fetched some sacking and wound it around his sculling blade, then at last got down into the dinghy and cast off.

The tide slid him down silently past the cutter. No one hailed him. He sat motionless, and the dinghy went like a dead leaf, quite slowly, crabwise to the tide. Two quiet strokes put her inshore of the *Maplin Bird,* then the yacht loomed up close and hid the dinghy from the guardian cutter. Toby could see no one on the *Bird*. She lay deserted, the light on her mast shining strongly. Toby stopped the dinghy with his oar and sculled her alongside. He caught the top of the bulwarks and sat still. His dinghy bumped the *Bird* with a hollow thud, but no one moved to investigate. He knew there was no one on board her.

He stood up and tied the dinghy alongside and shipped the oar. Then, delicate as a cat, he climbed on board and crouched down beside the hatch cover to take stock. No one had seen him. He was conscious of his own heart beating, but beyond that a blessed silence, a dispassionate nothingness all about him. The lights of Leigh looked ridiculously matter-of-fact across the water. Toby began to feel more confident. He crawled up to the mast and began to feel for the halyard cleats, to make quite sure of the arrangement so that when he set sail he could do it quickly. The rigging was immaculate, new and smooth, the mast had varnish on it like glass. Even in the darkness he could sense the quality of the *Maplin Bird,* and an excitement grew in him at the thought of sailing her. She was a thoroughbred, a wicked little beauty, and he wanted to feel her tiller pulling under his hand. There was nothing to stop him going now. He glanced around. The riding light shone coldly on him and he reached up and turned down the wick. The light guttered and went out and Toby held his breath. He was committed. He took out his knife, went forward, and started hacking through the mooring warp.

Now he was frightened, and slashed away savagely. As the last threads parted he caught the rope and broke its fall to the water so that only a ripple showed that the *Maplin Bird* was away. The tide eased her stern-first on the start of her journey. There was nothing in her path, and Toby hurried back aft, head down, to put her tiller over. He could not believe it was going to be so easy. His hand was sticky with sweat on the tiller and his heart seemed to be beating up in his throat.

"It can't be true," he thought. The lights on the cutter still shone doggedly; it lay silent although its little prisoner was already half a cable away. She was coming around, obedient to her rudder, and Toby left the tiller and went up forward to get up sail. He was going to wait until he thought she would be far enough away for the noise of flogging sheets to be out of earshot, but as he waited there by the mast, he heard what he had been expecting ever since he set foot on board.

A shout went up from the cutter.

"Ahoy! Ahoy, *Maplin Bird*."

He heard another shout and a rush of feet on the now distant cutter's deck, and he waited no longer. Grasping the halyard, he hauled away furiously. The staysail went up like a piece of silk. He ran back aft to sheet it in, and straightened the tiller as the yacht pointed her bowsprit for the open sea. Quick slashes of his knife freed the hampering dinghy, and sliced the sail tiers, then he was back at the mast to get up the mainsail. Now he was working feverishly. The wind brought him the grinding noise of the cutter's anchor coming aboard—he knew they were losing no time at all in getting under way. He could afford to waste no time in making canvas. The gaff climbed up against the dark sky, dragging up the vast red mainsail, billow upon fine billow of smoothest flax.

Toby swung on the throat, cleated down the peak halyard, and sweated up the throat another couple of inches until the luff was as taut as a bar. Then to the shrouds to slacken off the topping lift and aft like a monkey to trim the mainsheet. Loose sheets and halyard ends were coiled methodically: tidy work was the fastest work and Toby had learned the hard way. He worked like a race hand, strung up with a nervous tension that overlooked nothing, his pulse tingling with fear and his whole body flooded with a magnificent nervous exhilaration that he had never experienced before. With the jib out and the topsail straining, the *Maplin Bird* was truly flying. Toby's eyes were on the wind-hard curves of her lovely headsails and the great quivering belly of the freed-off mainsail that was the loveliest thing he had ever seen.

"No wonder he loves you," he said to her, thinking of Adam. "I wouldn't leave you to rot as revenue's loot either."

He thought of creaking *My Alice* with her frayed sheets and splintered decks, and wanted to laugh.

Suddenly a splash went up in the water beside him and a boom like thunder split the sky. Toby blinked. Almost immediately another boom followed. Toby's heart lurched.

"God, they're firing at us!"

It was a possibility that had never entered his head, and the fear that grasped him at the thought was more real than anything he had felt since meeting Adam. The *Maplin Bird* sped on, the water hustling behind her, white-laced in the darkness, but Toby's heart was no longer with her. He was strained for the sound of the gun and the deadly evidence of a little white splash. One of those little white splashes on target spelled death for the *Bird,* and very likely for him too, and he hadn't intended risking his life when he boarded the *Maplin Bird.* What was the cutter's range? He had no idea. She must be sailing now. Turning around, he could see her lights behind him but it was too dark to make out more than the half-light tower of her white sails. The night was moonless. He thought she was, perhaps a quarter of a mile away. But the accuracy of her shot suggested she was nearer.

The *Bird* was lifting her bowsprit to the sea and the water swilled up along her rail with a hiss that would have delighted Toby's heart a moment ago. The lights on Southend pier sparkled ahead, cosy and homely and mocking. Toby thought of Emily, wondered briefly how she had come to know of the *Maplin Bird,* and shuddered as another shot sounded. There was no splash this time, but the mainsail split just beneath the gaff and ripped down with what sounded to Toby like a scream. The *Bird* faltered like a winged gull. The brown curve was smashed to a torn, flying mass of useless ribbons. The gaff stood up ridiculously, holding nothing. The yacht slowed down perceptibly and Toby knew that her wild bid for freedom was over. They were both in trouble.

Mechanically he put the tiller over to head her clear of the pier. The foresails and the topsails were still pulling, for all the flogging mess that was her main driving power. But the cutter was nearer and her aim was bound to improve. Toby did not think she had finished with them. If he put her up into the wind would they accept the gesture as surrender? Or would he stand a chance of swimming for the pier? It was high water and the shore looked a long way away. The ebb would take him clear of the pier and he reckoned he would be drowned.

"If it comes to a choice, I'd rather be shot than drowned any day," he thought grimly and, as if in answer to his thoughts, he heard the whine of the shell that he knew, in one brief moment, spelled the end of the *Maplin Bird*. He even sensed that he saw it. He never heard the explosion for the heart-rending crunch and splinter of the spars above him. Mast, gaff, and rigging disintegrated. He remembered leaping to get clear, but the mangled, cracking mass was on him instantly. He was entangled and clouted, and, finally, hurt with a pain that drove all conscious thought out of his head. He saw the water very close and the torn red flax trailing. And no more.

Adam on the Run

Toby was extricated with some difficulty from the wreck of the *Maplin Bird* and taken aboard the big cutter. When neither buckets of sea water nor vigorous shaking could coax any sense out of him, the cutter was turned back to Leigh and the inert body rowed hastily ashore. Although it was scarcely dawn, the revenue officers had not been wrong in supposing that the little sortie had not gone unnoticed in Leigh. A surprising number of carefully nonchalant fishermen were down on the shore watching the approach of the rowing boat. The nonchalance was soon forgotten when it was seen who the prisoner was.

"Cor, what've you done to 'im? 'E's no smuggler. That's young Toby."

"You got the wrong man there, mates. Toby ain't done nothing. He's only a kid."

"That's my mate," Dick said astonished. "What you got 'im for? What happened?"

"Your young innocent took off in the *Maplin Bird,* that's what happened," said the officer tartly, "and we'd like to know what put the idea into his head. What do you know about it?"

Dick found himself surveyed closely by a pair of steely eyes.

"Nothing, sir," he said instinctively.

"Come on, think again."

"Cor, strike me! 'E didn't tell me anything. I was in 'The Peter Boat' all evening, didn't even see 'im."

"What was he doing then? Here, will this improve your memory?"

Dick saw the glint of a sovereign in the officer's hand and thought fast. He looked at Toby who was well beyond caring about the conversation bandying over his head, and hesitated. The sovereign was still in the officer's hand.

"He went to meet someone, but I don't know who."

"He told you he was going to meet someone?"

"He—" Dick paused, cleverly.

"He what?"

"He had a letter to say meet this person."

"Do you know who the letter was from?"

Dick hesitated again, until a second sovereign appeared in the officer's hand.

"It didn't say. Toby didn't know either."

"Why did he go then? There must have been something in it to make him go."

"Yes. It said the person was a friend of Toby's sister."

"His sister? Who's she? Where does she live?"

"Emily. I dunno where she lives."

"Don't you?"

There were three sovereigns now.

"It's worth thinking."

Dick thought so too. He wracked his memory.

"She's—she's a maid somewhere. In Southend somewhere. I think on the Royal Terrace—"

"Ah! What's the name of the people she works for? Can you remember? Remember that, and it's all yours." The officer turned the coins over in his palm. "Quickly."

"Seymour."

"Ah!" The exclamation was long-drawn out, loving. "Seymour. Adam Seymour."

The coins were in Dick's hand and the revenue officer was gone, striding rapidly away from the quay. Dick looked at Toby again. He was glad Toby was unconscious and had heard nothing of the conversation. He did not think Toby would have approved.

Emily got out of bed sleepily when Mrs. Briggs banged on her door. She scarcely felt she had been asleep at all with the night's disturbances still fresh in her mind: first Adam calling her up to get him some food when he came in at midnight and later, minutes after she had gone to sleep

again, the artillery banging away right outside her bedroom window. She had supposed that Adam, for some
devious reason, had wanted it known that he was home;
she could think of no other reason for his unusual behavior. As for the artillery, she didn't see why they couldn't
confine their exercises to their own territory off Shoebury,
instead of making all that commotion off the pier in
the middle of the night. She felt jaded. It was half-past
five, her normal hour of rising, but it felt to her more
like three. She washed in an inch of cold water, hurriedly
dressed and did her hair, and went downstairs, still tying
on her apron.

She was halfway down the last flight of stairs when a
knock sounded on the front door. It was a knock to wake
the entire household, and Emily gasped at its audacity.

"Heavens above! Whatever's happened? At this time in
the morning!"

Her numb brain registered only amazement. She walked
down the hall and opened the door. Standing on the doorstep were two customs officers, and in the road outside were
two more. Emily came awake as if she had been slapped in
the face.

"I have a warrant to take Mr. Adam Seymour into cus-
tody. Will you kindly inform him?"

The two officers stepped into the hall before Emily could
stop them. She retreated, staring wildly, groping for words.

"He—he—I don't know if—if he came home last night!
I'll call Mrs. Seymour. She—she will be able to tell you."

She turned and fled upstairs. The shock was so great that
all her breath seemed to have deserted her; her whole body
felt as if it were shaking. She paused momentarily outside
Adam's door, making an effort to pull herself together.

Then she knocked softly and, without waiting for an answer, went in.

"Sir, they—"

"They've come for me?" Adam was already out of bed. He had his trousers on and was rapidly buttoning his shirt, standing well away from the window. The curtains were undrawn.

"Have a look and see if they're guarding the back. Pretend to adjust the curtains."

He seemed perfectly composed. Emily stopped trembling and went to the window. At the bottom of the garden by the door which opened into the stable yard, she saw two men standing watching the house.

"It's no good. There are two men down there. And two in the road at the front." Emily had gathered her wits together. She thought of her own little room up in the roof. "Go upstairs," she said, "into the attic."

"I've no alternative. I can't go out and I can't go down. At least, I have no inclination that way. And they won't have the satisfaction of taking me in my nightshirt, whatever happens." Adam was rifling in the drawers of his desk, rapidly but not feverishly. He took out a small packet and passed it to Emily. "Put that in your pocket, will you? They're bound to search my room. Go and tell 'em I've gone out, then say your prayers for me, Emily my dear. You're the nicest maid my mother ever had."

Emily put the packet automatically into her apron pocket and watched Adam go out of the door. Her mouth was open and her eyes as round as marbles. Adam's words had completely scattered the self-control she had mastered with such difficulty, and she could only stare as he ran nimbly up the next flight of stairs. Mrs. Seymour, in a magnificent silk negligee, was coming down, and the two met face to face.

"Mother," Adam said, "you haven't seen me," and then he was past her and sprinting up the next flight of stairs to the attic. Mrs. Seymour's expression brought Emily back to earth. Its majestic scorn was withering.

"Emily, go and tell Miss Selina to get dressed. I fear we are going to be considerably disturbed."

Emily, already considerably disturbed herself, did as she was told. Selina, on inquiring and being told of the reason for her early awakening, yawned and said, "Good heavens! Whatever do they want with Adam?"

"He's a smuggler," Emily said, and had the satisfaction of seeing Selina's mouth drop open as if she had been shot. Emily retreated before Selina had found words, and stood for a moment, listening for any sound of Adam upstairs. But all was silence. Quickly she went downstairs and into Adam's room, where she hastily straightened the bed and put the quilt over it and scooped his clothes into the closet. Then, feeling that there was nothing else she could do to help, she went out and shut the door. The men were already coming up the stairs.

"Which is Mr. Seymour's room?"

"This one, sir."

"Was he home last night?"

"I don't know, sir."

Had Mrs. Seymour lied for Adam, Emily wondered? They must have asked her the same question.

"Stay here with us," the officer snapped. He had opened the door and seen that the room was empty. "Get Smith

and Arnold to come in and help search," he ordered the
other man. "Brown can guard the front. We've no time to
waste if he's not here."

He went into the room and flung open all the cupboard
and closet doors, upended the drawers and sorted through
the contents. He found the brandy in the bookcase, emptied
the desk so that papers went flying, flung open the bed and
examined the mattress, the pillows, the floorboards, and the
skirtings. Meanwhile the other men had come upstairs and
were rapidly going through each room looking for Adam.
Emily stood on the landing, tense with apprehension. The
officer, apparently disgusted with his lack of success in
Adam's room, hurried up to the next floor and Emily followed. The women's bedrooms—with a horrified Selina
still in bed—were checked and the party moved up the last
flight of stairs to the attic.

"What's up here?" the officer asked her briskly.

"Only the maids' rooms, sir," Emily answered. She stood
on the tiny landing, trying to look as if she didn't care, and
wondering feverishly where Adam had got to. Dark cupboards full of gurgling cisterns were explored, the rafters
prodded, the storeroom turned out, and the two bedrooms
scoured. Emily stood dumbly, dreading to see Adam pulled
out like a hunted animal, too afraid to enjoy the officer's
anger when the dark caves in the roof proved fruitless
and the rooms empty. She moved forward breathlessly and
looked into her own room. The corner of the faded cotton curtain was caught in the closed window. She noted it
quickly and moved her eyes away carefully, scared to show
any change in her expression. She felt she hardly dared
breathe. The searchers were angry and boxes and furniture shook the floor; in their haste they did not trouble

to respect Mrs. Seymour's possessions. Emily could see her employer's upturned face, grim as granite, on the landing below, and Mrs. Briggs looking demented, wringing her red hands and rolling her eyes at the unseemliness of the whole operation.

"He must be away," the officer said, when Mrs. Briggs's room revealed nothing. "We'll go down to Shoebury and see if we can pick him up there. He must have made arrangements to take over the *Bird* somewhere out in the estuary, so we've a chance if we're quick."

The withdrawal was as sudden and precipitous as the arrival. The men clattered down the stairs, nodded to the speechless Mrs. Briggs, bid good morning to Mrs. Seymour, and hurried out into the street. Emily went downstairs slowly, feeling slightly sick. Her knees were trembling. Mrs. Seymour's face had changed. She looked as human as Emily had ever seen her, her mouth shaking like a child's.

"Where is Adam?" she asked Emily.

"He's on the roof, ma'am."

"See if the men have gone, then shut the front door."

The street was empty. A drizzle of rain came in on the breeze. Emily shut the door and bolted it. When she turned around Mrs. Seymour had overcome her frailty and her eyes were like flints.

"When Adam comes down," she said to Emily—as if coming down from the chimney pots was a perfectly normal occurrence—"tell him I want him to join me for breakfast. Mrs. Briggs, breakfast in fifteen minutes please. Hot water at once, Emily, and for Mr. Adam."

Emily guessed that Adam would have almost preferred to go with the customs men than have breakfast with his mother. She went down to the kitchen with Mrs. Briggs who was on the verge of hysteria. Emily felt weak, as if she had already done her day's work.

"God save us, who ever'd have thought—!" Mrs. Briggs choked. "Mr. Adam in trouble! I could have guessed he was up to no good, all that coming and going in the small hours, but I never thought—oh, mercy, poor Mrs. Seymour! However will she live this down? Who ever'd have thought. . . ."

Emily drew her hot water in silence and left her rambling on, hammering the china onto Mrs. Seymour's breakfast tray and sniffing noisily over the stove. She was wondering what had set the customs men on to Adam at this late stage in his shady career. They had had the *Maplin Bird* in their hands for several days now, yet had not been on to him before. He had gone out last night at eight, immediately after dinner, and had seemed exhilarated and excited when he came home. Emily was puzzled. Something that he had done last night had been his undoing. What was it?

Adam was coming down the stairs. He was covered with grime and looked worried. As well he might, Emily thought grimly. He paused in the doorway of his room, looking at the shambles the men had left.

"It could be worse," he said, scratching his head reflectively. "But not much," he added softly.

Emily, now that the alarms were over, felt a perverse anger toward Adam for causing such an upheaval in her emotions. She stepped over the things strewn across the floor and set the heavy jug on the washstand with a thump worthy of Mrs. Briggs.

"Mrs. Seymour wants you to join her for breakfast in fifteen minutes, sir," she told him.

A look of apprehension came into Adam's face. "Yes, I'll bet she does," he said bitterly. He ran a hand miserably through his disheveled hair and added absently, "Find me some clothes amongst this assortment."

The white starched shirts that Emily spent so many of her afternoons laboriously ironing were scattered all around the room, along with letters, books, riding boots, ledgers, ornaments, and various bric-à-brac from the desk and mantelshelf. Adam started to shave and Emily laid his clothes on the bed. He said nothing, in spite of all that had happened, and Emily knew she could ask him no questions. His eyes were angry in the mirror, and his hand none too steady. He cut himself, and swore softly. Emily withdrew, shutting the door quietly, and went back downstairs. A watery sun was beginning to filter through the fanlight above the front door. It was still early; the street was silent, and Emily had a feeling that the disordered house was brooding over the day's revelations. There was nobody in it at peace with the world. The atmosphere was nervous. The dust jumped in the sunlight, and the clocks ticked inexorably. Emily knew that Adam would be caught, and she thought he knew it too, sometime.

Mrs. Seymour came down in a silver-gray morning dress, every hair in place beneath her lace cap. Adam came down impeccably tidy, and grave.

"Good morning, Mother."

"Good morning, Adam."

Emily brought in the breakfast and served it neatly. Everything was in place, to the last engraved napkin ring. Emily could hear the crackle of her own apron, and the buzzing of a fly against the window pane and she could feel Mrs. Seymour waiting for her to go, and Adam wishing that she could be all day arranging the teapot on its silver stand. She straightened his knife. His hands looked very brown against the white cloth; they were sailor's hands, with callouses like Toby's.

"That will be all, Emily."

"Yes, m'm."

She went out, and Mrs. Briggs told her to start tidying up. She went up to Adam's room and set to work to put everything back in its place. But all she could think of was Mrs. Seymour's stony face and her disappointed eyes. She didn't think Adam would enjoy his breakfast very much. It lasted a long time, as she guessed it would, and the voices were very quiet and controlled. When the bell rang at last for her to clear away and she went into the room, the same silence enmeshed her. The china clattered on the tray. Mrs. Seymour sat very straight and silent, looking out of the window, and Adam stood scowling by the fireplace, but neither said a word. When she had filled the tray, Adam opened the door for her. He followed her out and went up to his room, and Emily carried the tray downstairs to the kitchen where Mrs. Briggs was regaling the impressed Mrs. Noakes with the tale of the morning's alarms.

"What are they doing, love?" Mrs. Noakes asked her when she came in. "Laying into each other or being dignified like?"

"They were being very quiet," Emily said.

"Mrs. Seymour's worst when she's quiet," Mrs. Briggs said. "They haven't eaten much either. Not that that surprises me. Can't say as I shall have much appetite for the rest of the day either."

"Mr. Adam won't think much of prison food. 'E should make the best of 'is meals while 'e can," Mrs. Noakes said.

"Well, I don't know, but I never wished him in prison,

although I've said plenty of unkind things about him in my time," Mrs. Briggs said.

"He's not there yet," Emily pointed out.

"He'll get what's coming to 'im. Look, 'e's ringing, love. Go and see what he wants." Mrs. Noakes might as well have added, "And let us know afterward," for the suggestion was implicit in her voice.

Emily knew that Adam would be going away. There was nothing else for him, and she was not surprised to see that he had changed into his riding clothes and was shrugging into the well-used black coat. His boots were still covered with dust from the night before. He took a pair of spurs down from where they hung on the gas bracket and strapped them on. He didn't usually wear spurs, Emily had noticed.

"You rang, sir?" she said.

He straightend up and looked at her. He looked miserable and anxious and not a bit like the intrepid thorn in the flesh of the British Customs and Excise.

"Yes," he said. "I'm going now and I want you to go down to the stable and just see that there's nobody watching the back. I doubt if there will be now, but we might as well make sure." He looked rather absently around the room. "I'm not taking anything. And I don't know when I'll be back. I've said good-bye to my mother, so there's nothing more. . . ." His eyes came back to her and rested on her face. "You might find out, very soon, that I'm more of a sinner than you know at the moment. If you do, I'm sorry, Emily," he said.

"What do you mean?" Emily asked.

"You'll see," Adam said. "Just remember that I'm sorry, that's all. I would give anything, now, for last night not to have happened. As it is. . . ." He shrugged. "The mistakes are all made. The damage is done. Remember that I'm sorry, Emily."

"I don't know what you mean. Not why you should say it to me, at least. Your mother, perhaps."

"You will," Adam said.

Emily looked at him uneasily. But before she could ask for any more explanations he turned away and said, "Go along now. Tell Gregory to saddle the mare quickly if it's clear, and give me a wave from the gate. I'll be watching for you."

"Yes, sir."

He opened the long window for her and she hurried down the iron staircase into the garden. His words had puzzled her and filled her with an uneasy fear; they were meaningless to her, yet apparently important to him. Whatever it was she was going to find out, it sounded unpleasant. But she was at the gate and into the back of the mews. Gregory was grooming, and the sweet smell of hay and horses brought her mind back to business. The old man straightened up and said, "What's been going on around here this morning?"

"Mr. Adam sent me to see if anyone's watching the back. The revenue officers called to arrest him this morning."

Gregory whistled. "So that's it! They're on to him at last, eh? Gave 'em the slip, did he?"

"Yes. He hid on the roof. Is there anyone still watching? He wants to go if the coast's clear."

"They've all gone now, as far as I know. Wait a moment. I'll have a look."

Gregory walked to both ends of the narrow mews street, but saw no sign of anything unusual, so while Emily went to give Adam the signal he set about saddling Adam's mare.

"Good job she's fit," he said to Emily when she came back. "He was galloping around half the night on her. The feed she puts away! She'd jump out of her own hoofs if she belonged to anyone who used her properly. . . ."

The mare was a dark bay with a small, nervous head and white-rimmed eye.

"I bet he'll set you a galloping today, old girl," Gregory said.

Adam came into the stable and took the mare out into the street. He tightened the girth a hole, then got up into the saddle.

"Good luck, sir," Gregory said.

"Thank you." Adam looked at Emily, watching from the doorway. "Good-bye, Emily. Don't think too badly of me, afterward."

Emily shook her head. At that moment she didn't think she could ever think badly of Adam. He trotted away down the street, reined the mare into the main road at the end, and disappeared. Gregory grinned broadly at Emily.

"You a friend of Mr. Adam's, eh?"

"How can I be? I'm only the maid."

"Wouldn't be the first maid he's been friends with, believe me," Gregory said. He turned back into the stable and surveyed the mare's empty stall. "I don't suppose I shall be seeing her again in a hurry. Nor you, Mr. Adam, come to that."

"No."

Emily went back through the gateway and up the garden to the kitchen.

A Carriage for Toby

When Emily got back to the kitchen Mrs. Briggs had her breakfast waiting for her. She felt numb and wretched, and grateful for five minutes' peace in the kitchen, with a plate of porridge and a mug of tea. She answered Mrs. Noakes's questions in monosyllables, and Mrs. Briggs gave her a sharp look and said, "What are *you* moping for, miss? Anyone'd think it was you they're after."

Mrs. Noakes gave one of her broad winks and said, "Feels the same, dear. Don't you know she's sweet on Mr. Adam?"

Emily said nothing. For all she knew, Mrs. Noakes was right. She had never before felt the soreness that was inside her now, and there was no reason for it, apart from Mrs. Noakes's. If it was true, her own stupidity appalled her. The realization was worse than the pain.

"I'll sweeten her, if there's any of that nonsense," Mrs. Briggs said grimly.

"Oh, go on, Mrs. Briggs. If you were twenty years younger now—"

Forty, Emily thought.

"When I was a girl I knew my place."

So do I, Emily thought, burying her face in the damp gloom of the tea mug. She felt like crying.

A loud rap on the front door startled the two women out of their exchanges. Emily got to her feet but Mrs. Briggs said, "I'll see to it. Sit down."

"It's only just gone seven now," Mrs. Noakes said. "It can't be anyone normal. Probably that lot back again. Lucky Mr. Adam went when he did."

"I don't see that they can want any more here now."

But Mrs. Briggs came back and reported otherwise. "It's you they want now, miss," she said to Emily. "They're in the morning room with Mrs. Seymour."

Emily was shocked out of her apathy.

"Me! What do they want with me?"

"Yes, that's what I'd like to know," Mrs. Briggs said. "Get along now. I've no doubt you'll find out soon enough."

Emily was frightened. She hurried up the stairs, trying to think of anything she mustn't say to incriminate Adam. But her mind was in utter confusion. She was panting with nervousness, and stopped outside the door to gather her wits. But it opened suddenly and the officer she had seen earlier was standing there. He looked angry.

"Come in, girl."

Mrs. Seymour, now quite composed, was sitting in her usual chair, and another officer stood in the window, looking out to sea. He turned around when she entered, and Mrs. Seymour said, "Come in, Emily. These gentlemen want to ask you some questions."

Emily made a great effort to look as unworried as possible and said, "Yes, m'm." She went and stood by the breakfast table that she had served such a short while before and the officer sat down and looked at her across its shining expanse.

"Now, Emily." He did not sound angry any more. Emily decided he was being clever, and hoped she could be clever too. But his first question caught her off her guard.

"Did you know anything about the meeting between Mr. Seymour and your brother, Toby Garland, last night?"

Emily felt as if he had hit her. "My brother! What do you mean? He has nothing to do with all this!"

"He has, you know," the officer said, gently. He was watching her very carefully, but Emily was no longer concerned with being clever.

"He's not in trouble?" Emily asked. "He's all right?"

"Depends what you mean by trouble," the officer said. "I don't think we'll be prosecuting him, if that's what you mean. But we want his part in this little matter cleared up."

"I didn't know he had a part in it," Emily said vehemently. "And if he has, it's only just recently. He's not been mixed up in Mr. Seymour's—activities."

"But he met Mr. Seymour last night. You didn't know that?"

"No, I didn't. But if he did, it was for the first time."

"How do you know?"

"Because Mr. Seymour only asked me about my brother a day or two ago—the day the *Maplin Bird* was brought in. He said then he'd like to meet him, but I don't know why."

"Your brother can sail a boat, that's why. However . . . you didn't arrange this meeting?"

"No, I did not. I didn't want Mr. Seymour to have anything to do with my brother."

"No, I can understand that. You knew what Mr. Seymour was up to then?"

"Yes, sir."

"How long have you known?"

It seemed forever. Emily couldn't think. "I—I don't know. A few weeks perhaps."

"How did you find out?"

Emily explained how the little model had given Adam away, and how Toby had told her that the *Maplin Bird* was the smuggler's boat. As she spoke she was wondering wildly what Toby had done last night, what had gone wrong? What was it that Adam would have given anything not to have done? His strange apologies were all beginning to make sense. She could not bear not to know.

"Please, sir, what has happened to Toby? What happened last night? Is he all right?"

"He attempted to sail the *Maplin Bird* out from under our noses," the officer said. "He all but succeeded too, but he didn't bargain for our firing on him. We stopped the *Bird* and your brother too. We didn't kill him, child," he added sharply, at the look on Emily's face. "His leg's broken. He'll survive."

"Oh! The firing was. . . ." Emily's voice choked into silence. She could not express her bitterness at what had happened. That Adam had chosen Toby—of all people— to do such a dangerous task! The troubled look in Adam's eyes as he had told her, "Don't think too badly of me, afterward," . . . why ever hadn't she realized what he was warning her of? Who else had she to care about? Only Toby. Emily could not trust herself to speak. She turned to Mrs. Seymour in desperation.

"I don't think either the girl or her brother can be reproached for anything they've done," Mrs. Seymour was saying. "My son is entirely to blame. I've no doubt he bribed the boy. You won't charge the lad?"

"No, ma'am," said the officer. "And I'm satisfied that this girl was not an accomplice. That's all I wanted to know. Your son now—that's another matter. . . ." He sniffed.

"I understand that. Have you finished?"

"Yes, ma'am, for the time being."

Mrs. Seymour rang for Mrs. Briggs to show the two officers out. As soon as they had gone she said to Emily, "I shall see that your brother is taken care of. Don't worry. I think you had better go to see him, to relieve your mind. I shall tell Mrs. Briggs that you are to have the day off, and Gregory will take you to wherever it is in the gig."

"Thank you, ma'am." The offer would have astonished Emily if she had been in a clearer frame of mind. But in her head were the reverberations of the shooting the night before, the muffled wretched echoes thudding against the sandy cliffs. She felt as if the explosions had shattered her sanity. She could think of nothing but Toby, mangled and bloody, amongst that hideous noise.

"Sit down," Mrs. Seymour was saying. "Calm yourself. I will send Mrs. Briggs to fetch your shawl and bonnet, and tell Gregory to prepare the gig immediately."

Mrs. Seymour, serene and in command, seemed to have no troubles of her own. Emily found herself sitting on one of the best chairs and blowing her nose on Mrs. Seymour's own embroidered handkerchief while Mrs. Briggs ran to fetch her things and take the message to Gregory. In a very short time she was in the gig and on her way, but the sudden splendor of her unexpected situation behind the gleaming tail of Fanny, the gig horse, was hard to appreciate. She felt stupid with shock and worry. The surprised Gregory asked her where they were going, but Emily told him to put her down by the church. She could run down to the cottage where Toby lived in a matter of minutes; she didn't fancy arriving in such a conspicuous manner outside the cottage door. Gregory asked no questions, but Emily had a feeling he knew what was happening, as, earlier, she thought he had known all about Adam's activities.

It was a fine morning after the early rain, but Emily felt that the sunshine was a mockery as she ran down the cobbled steps beside the church. Gregory had said he would wait, but Emily had no idea what she would find at Dick's cottage, or what she would have to do. There was nothing to show that anything out of the ordinary had happened in Leigh that morning; women were beating their mats and pounding their tubs of washing and the men were smoking on the sea wall, waiting for the tide; a fleet of collier brigs was bowling up toward Canvey and the cockles were boiling in the cockle sheds. All was as it should be. Emily was shivering.

Dick was standing in the doorway of his home, and looked startled when he saw her.

"You heard, then?"

"Where's Toby?"

"In bed." Dick jerked his head inside the cottage and moved over to let her in. "Don't know what he thinks he's up to, larking about with the *Maplin Bird*. Fair old rumpus we had down here this morning."

Emily didn't listen to him, but hurried into the dark cottage. A stench of neglect, of stale boiled fish and musty floors and peeling damp met her nostrils. Dirty crockery littered the table inside the door and a fire in the range smoked miserably. Dick followed her in and pointed to a door that led into a small storeroom. It had a small window high up in the wall like a larder and was full of sails and warps, save for a space against a wall where a truckle bed stood. On the bed, looking blessedly whole and unmangled, lay Toby.

"Toby! Oh, Toby, what's wrong with you? What've you been doing? Are you all right?"

"No, he's not all right. He's broken his leg. Haven't you, you young idiot?" Dick said conversationally.

Toby sent Dick a look full of loathing and contempt. He lay fully dressed on the bed with a dirty blanket thrown over him. His face was drawn in a way Emily had never seen before, and there were beads of sweat on his forehead.

"Is it true?" Emily said to him. "Can't you walk?"

Toby shook his head.

"It's a right old mess," Dick said, leaning in the doorway.

"But what are you going to do about it?" Emily said helplessly.

"Ma said she'd tie it up when she comes in," Dick said.

"If she's not too drunk," Toby muttered.

"Can't you get a doctor?" Emily said to Dick. Dick looked at her as if she were mad.

"What for? Pay for that old sawbones? Ma can manage. She done me up when I hurt my arm."

Emily straightened up and looked slowly around the room. In the last few weeks she had grown unaccustomed to filth and mismanagement as she saw it in Dick's home. Toby, flung helplessly on the dirty bed, was as much refuse as the torn staysail she had her foot on. Dick's family had taken Toby in; she thought they were kind, but now she saw that they did not care, indeed scarcely noticed, another person in their muddled, drink-sodden existence. Dick's mother had come in now and was trying to draw up the smoking fire in the kitchen. She looked to Emily like a witch at her caldron. Her hands trembled, and a stream of steady blasphemy came from her lips. The thought of her putting a hand on Toby made Emily want to retch.

She bent down and said to Toby, "Are you all right— for a little while? I'm going to ask Mrs. Seymour if I can come and stay with you, and I'll find a doctor to see to your leg. I shan't be long. You can't stay like this."

"All right." It was an effort for him to speak.

Emily turned round and saw Dick looking at her derisively.

"Haughty wench," he said.

Emily fled back up the hill.

Emily had never thought she would ask Mrs. Seymour for help, nor find that forbidding face kindly and the stern eyes sympathetic. In the last five hours the world seemed to have turned upside down.

"Well, what did you find?"

Mrs. Seymour was drinking coffee in the morning room, with Selina this time. Selina, at least had made a good breakfast, and she looked more animated than usual. She looked cautiously at Emily, who tried to explain the condition in which she had found Toby. How could Mrs. Seymour know what Dick's cottage was like? Emily knew her words were conveying little. She could not explain the look in Toby's eyes and Dick's malice.

"But if you will let me, ma'am, I would like to go and look after him till he's better." The appeal was plain enough.

Mrs. Seymour did not reply at once. She drank some coffee and put her cup down carefully. Then she said, "But I cannot do without you, Emily."

"I must go."

"I do not think it's a good idea. The place you describe is hardly suitable for a sick person. We have a spare room here. I think you should bring him home."

Emily's mouth dropped open. She was so astonished she could say nothing.

Mrs. Seymour went on, "And you have more than enough to do without turning nurse. Selina shall look after him."

This time it was Selina who was shaken. She turned an appalled face out of her coffee cup.

"Mama!"

"You have been telling me how badly you want to be a

nurse. It's all you've been talking about since Christmas. Very well, you shall have your way."

"But, Mama! He—he's common—"

"Sick people are often common. And no one believe me, is as common as a criminal. Think of your own brother."

Emily found herself exchanging glances with Selina. In that moment they were equally shattered by Mrs. Seymour's decision, so that in their glances mutual astonishment formed a bond. Emily thought Mrs. Seymour had lost her senses to make such a suggestion, and it was plain that Selina thought the same.

"If Gregory takes the carriage, do you think your brother will be able to get in? The step is not very high. He could be lifted."

Emily nodded faintly.

"I shall ask Mrs. Briggs to make the bed up. You will have no more to worry about, Emily. You, Selina, can go and ask Dr. Spencer to call."

She rang the bell for Mrs. Briggs. Once more Emily found herself traveling back to Leigh, this time in the carriage. When Gregory drove it down the narrow street to halt in front of Dick's cottage, a crowd quickly gathered. Gregory organized several volunteers to transfer Toby to the carriage and in a short time they were traveling back to Southend. Dick, like Emily, had been too surprised to pass any remarks. Emily, crouched by Toby in the carriage, her teeth on edge at the jolting, told Toby of Mrs. Seymour's plan. He gave her a look of horror every bit as eloquent as Selina's and lapsed into unconsciousness. And Emily envied him his tranquillity.

Selina Surprises

There was something that Emily had forgotten in the confusion of the day. When she went to bed that night she remembered the package that Adam had thrust at her and she had dropped into her apron pocket. The apron thudded as it slipped to the floor. Curious, Emily picked up the packet and opened it. It was a necklace of blue opals.

"Oh!"

Emily held it up. In the candlelight the stones revealed their strange milky flames and spikes of color, stones "as big as bird's eggs." The phrase came back to Emily vividly. She pretended that she was shocked but an inner sense told her that she had known all along. To be shocked was to lie to herself. "He's callous and dishonest. He wasn't worth hiding and helping and caring about. He was the 'Southend shark' and that little black yacht at anchor was the *Maplin Bird*. I knew it all the time."

She was too tired to cry, but with the opening of the packet she felt as if her world had no bottom in it at all. The night was quiet and warm. The lights of a passing ship spangled the flooding tide and the moths burred in the frayed curtains. But Emily could think of nothing nice in the whole world. She blew out the candle and got between her stiff sheets and lay looking up at the tangled roses on the sloping ceiling above her head. It wasn't dark; somewhere there was a moon, but she hadn't noticed it. The day's kaleidoscope in her head was in dark patterns, disaster upon disaster, but mercifully she was incapable of staying awake to think about them. She went to sleep with the opals under her pillow.

In the guest room below, Toby was not so lucky. He lay awake, sleepless not so much from pain as from the astonishment at the events of the last twenty-four hours. The bed with its crackling sheets and embroidered quilt, the high ceiling with its gilt cornice glimmering in the moonlight were as unreal to him as his unhappy escapade with the *Maplin Bird*. The strangeness would not let him relax. The only familiar thing he could see was the sea outside the long window, with a few lights shining far out on the Kent coast and a red navigation lamp moving out on the tide, and he kept his eyes turned that way for comfort. There was little comfort anywhere else, either in the disastrous past or the uncertain future. He remembered only disjointed, agonized fragments of the day, but of the small hours at the tiller of the *Maplin Bird* he could recall every breath and every fatal detail. It still seemed very close, almost as if he was out there now.

"Poor little ship," he thought. The gun had made a mess of them both, shattering spars and bones alike, as well as the comfortless orderly routine that had become his life. Toby did not think about what was to become of him now, stranded like a freak in this satin-quilted bed. He wished Emily was there to talk to. He had wanted her that morning when the doctor had changed out of his morning coat into a blood-caked overall like a beef slaughterer and told Selina that he didn't use anesthetic on the working classes. Selina had fetched some smelling salts, but for her own use, not his. Toby had wanted the familiarity of Emily, not Selina's tight, disgusted face; even the drunken compassion of Dick's mother would have been preferable (and she at least would have seen him well laced with gin). Toby was doubtful about the advantages of this superior nursing. Like Emily, he could see nothing good in the immediate future.

Neither of them were mistaken in their prophecies. Two black weeks followed. Emily was expected to go about her work as usual; Toby's presence in the house was apparently no concern of hers, only of Selina's. But she could hardly remain ignorant of the fact that Toby was dangerously ill, that his leg had become gangrenous, as she had dreaded it would, and that while she beat the mats and polished the brass the doctor was upstairs discussing with Selina his fears of saving the limb. Emily could not bring herself to think of what each day would bring. And the fact that it was Adam who had brought this fate to her incautious brother caused her the bitterest reflections of all: Adam whom she had protected in her poor silly way, who had been sorry but who had vanished before she had learned why. No word came from him, but neither was there any news of his capture.

In a strange way, the routine of the house continued unchanged, the chores were still to be done, the meals to be served, the linen to be mended, the water to be carried; yet in no one's mind, Emily thought, was life the same at all. Mrs. Seymour was now an anxious old woman, rather than a forbidding one. Her face was visibly thinner and a little twitch came sadly to the corner of her lip at times. Mrs. Briggs was bad-tempered at their shattered respectability, finding that it rubbed off on herself. The scandal of the Seymour household was currently the most important item of gossip in all the kitchens along the terrace (not to mention, doubtless, the drawing rooms) and Mrs. Briggs took angry exception to her reflected notoriety. Mrs. Noakes loved it. Only Selina had found any profit in the situation, and that to everyone's astonishment. Emily hated her for it.

After her first reaction of horror, Selina had become a completely selfless nurse. She asked no one for help, coming down to the kitchen herself to prepare invalid meals or fetch water. She never complained, in fact she never said anything at all, but went about looking (Emily thought) disgustingly self-sufficient and unflustered. Emily knew that she herself was jealous, but this perspicacity gave her no joy. She hated stuck-up Selina for being the one to watch over Toby, she hated her competence, her quiet air of possession, her beastly devotion. But the fact that Selina the self-indulgent, Selina the sulk, was indeed proving competent had to be admitted.

"It's a bloomin' miracle," said Mrs. Noakes. "Life's nothing but surprises these days, eh, Emily?"

Emily preferred her life without surprises. She nodded miserably.

"I must say, I hadn't expected it of Miss Selina," said Mrs. Briggs grimly.

Their admiration was grudging, for they resented Selina in the kitchen. She did not ask for advice in what she was doing, only the whereabouts of the wooden spoons, or a strainer; otherwise she moved from the range to the scullery and from the scullery to the table in silence. She wore her soberest dresses and a starched apron, and Mrs. Noakes warned Gregory to look carefully before he shouted for

his drink at the back door in case he got a bowl of gruel from Miss Nightingale herself. She never asked Emily if she wanted to see Toby; she never spoke to her at all, not even to say how Toby was, and it was Emily who had to ask after him, trying to keep the anxiety out of her voice. Selina's replies were hardly calculated to give joy.

"He's as well as can be expected, considering the pig-headed ignorance of Dr. Spencer."

"Whatever did she mean by that?" Emily implored in the kitchen.

"She means she told Dr. Spencer what to do," Mrs. Noakes said. "And he didn't take any notice."

"What does she know about it then?"

"She knows what her boy friend told her. The one from Edinburgh. He's a student up there, and it seems that his professor's patients don't die after an operation nearly as often as everyone else's. Something he's invented, I suppose. Or just luck. Don't ask me dearie. Ask Miss Selina. You didn't meet her boy friend, did you? He set her off on this nurse and good works business. She wasn't nearly so much trouble before she met him, was she, Mrs. Briggs?"

"No, that's a fact. Pity he ever came home."

"Well, she seems to be doing all right now. Better *doing* than flying into tantrums all day."

"A bit of hard work never hurt no one."

"Run the fat off her."

In fact Selina never said anything in the kitchen because she didn't know how to meet servants on their own ground. Silence was her defense. And Emily she preferred to avoid, because Emily's fierce intelligence put her at a loss. An intelligent housemaid was a contradiction in terms, in Selina's limited experience, and Emily unnerved Selina. She did not want to meet her scornful eyes, nor see the belligerent set of her lovely jawline. No wonder, Selina thought, Adam had admired Emily. But even he had the sense to see that she wasn't the sort of maid whose behind one patted in the passage.

Emily saw Toby when at last the ignorant Dr. Spencer had pronounced him out of danger, whole, and on the road to complete recovery. The announcement made her so happy that she was quite prepared to embrace Selina for her maligned devotion. Selina, however, left them alone;

when Emily went in, she went out. Emily hardly recognized
Toby.

"Toby! Mercy on us, is it really you?"

"Why, who do you think it is?"

"King Toby, I should have said. King Tobias of Royal
Terrace. How clean you are! Oh, Toby, I've been so worried!"

"Not half as worried as I've been."

He was as pale as the proverbial lily, but as much from
mere lack of weatherbeatenness as from ill health. Emily
had never seen him looking so civilized, so clean, his hair so
tidy, his hands so white and idle-looking. He looked no
more like a fisherman than the Prince Consort. She stared
at him in awe.

"You look a proper toff. Cor, *My Alice* won't know you
after this! So delicate! So elegant! Oh, Toby!"

It was hard to believe that she didn't have to worry about
him any more. She had to laugh, although the relief of
seeing him again made her feel ridiculously like crying.

"How do you feel? How long have you got to stay in
bed?"

"I dunno. Till I can walk all right, I suppose. Where've
you been all this time? I feel I've been here a year already.
I've been worried about things—I wanted to talk to you."
He propped himself up on an elbow and looked at her
anxiously. Emily noticed that he was wearing one of
Adam's nightshirts, and the sight gave her a strange pang.
"I suppose they've been looking after the smack for me,
although she should be lying snug enough. But I lost the
rowing boat that night, and it might've come ashore somewhere. I must try and get it back. Then there's the money
Mr. Seymour gave me. I hid it in a mattress on *My Alice*.

Whether it's still there or not. . . ." He shrugged. "I reckon I earned it. I don't want to lose it."

"How much was it?"

He told her. "There'd have been more if I'd got away."

"Oh, he was wicked to ask you!" Emily said, her indignation welling up. "To get *you* into trouble—"

"I didn't have to go, did I? I chose." Toby looked at her sternly. "It was lucky I didn't still have it on me, else they'd have fleeced me for sure. They had the chance easy enough."

"You're lucky you didn't land in prison."

"Oh, yes, I was lucky a lot of ways. I wish I was mended now though."

He looked wistfully toward the window. Emily noticed that the bed had been moved to improve his view. "Is there any chance of you going down to Leigh—to see about the rowing boat, and get the money?"

"If the money's still there, it'll keep a little longer, won't it?" Emily said. "I've not got a day off for another fortnight." She had no wish to handle Adam's bribe; the idea of the money disgusted her. And she had no wish to meet Dick again either.

"Another fortnight? I suppose that will have to do. I might be out of bed by then. Oh, two weeks feels like two years cooped up here! Emmy, it's been so strange. I wished I could have seen you lots of times."

"Miss Selina doesn't seem to approve of visiting. I was always asking after you, and worrying, but she never asked me up."

"She's a queer wench." Toby said softly. "But all right. She's done for me all right, and it wasn't easy. I don't know why she bothers so. I've plenty to be grateful for."

As Toby improved, Emily saw him more often. Generally she managed to slip in when Selina wasn't there, but as time went by she began to get the impression that Selina made some excuse to come in when she heard their voices. At first Emily felt uncomfortable in her presence. She suspected that Selina was spying on her precious moments with Toby, and when Selina was in the room she felt tongue-tied and resentful. But Toby seemed to have no such inhibitions. Although his manner was respectful, he spoke to Selina easily. And in Selina's acceptance of Toby, Emily was reminded of her own strange relationship with Adam. The whole sequence of events since she had discovered Adam's true vocation never ceased to astonish her, and this latest development she found equally surprising. As Mrs. Noakes had said, "Life's nothing but surprises these days."

One evening she went up to the guest room an hour before dinner, having hurried with her tasks to spare half an hour with Toby. But when she went in she saw that Toby was asleep. She hesitated in the doorway, and would have gone away, but Selina was sitting in the window working at some embroidery. Before Emily could retreat, Selina said, "Don't go away. It's time he was waking up. If Mrs. Briggs has spared you, you can wait awhile."

"Thank you, miss." Emily shut the door smartly, hoping it would wake Toby up, but he only stirred slightly and went on sleeping, while Selina continued with her sewing. Emily stood uncertainly by the bed, not knowing what to do. Selina said nothing. She was wearing one of her plain, dark dresses and her hair was done up at the back of her head in a dark mass as simply as Emily's own. Along with her new severity of appearance, she had a serenity Emily had never noticed before. Emily watched her nervously.

She found she no longer felt any resentment toward her; in fact, glancing at Toby and recognizing again the care that had been lavished on him, she suddenly said what she knew she should have said long ago.

"Miss Selina, thank you for being so good to Toby." She felt herself going red as soon as the words were out, but Selina was flushing too.

"You've nothing to thank me for, Emily. There's nothing else I'd rather have done."

"It can't have been easy for you, miss." Emily was remembering Selina's horror at the breakfast table when her mother had first put forward the idea.

"Not at first. Toby had more courage than I had. But now—oh, now I keep wondering what I'm going to do when he's better! I shall go mad!" Selina flung down her sewing and leaped up from her seat as if it had stung her. "Oh, Emily, if only you knew what it is to feel useful after all these years! You can never guess. You—*you* are almost killed with work, and I am killed with boredom. It is insufferable!"

The serenity had gone. Emily, appalled, looked anxiously toward Toby, willing him to wake up and cause a diversion, but Selina was not concerned at that moment with her patient. "No wonder Adam turned to being a pirate!" she went on. "He was bored, and yet what excuse had he compared to me? I might as well be dead as sit my life out here. Oh, Emily, what I'd give to go away, to learn something and do something! You don't know how I envy you at times! I have no more freedom to choose what I want to do than you do, and so much more time to spend regretting it."

Emily did not know what to say. She had never thought

to have Selina's confidence imparted to her as well as Adam's, and felt completely inadequate to venture a reply. She looked dumbly at Selina.

"What would you do, Emily, if you could choose?" Selina asked her.

Emily floundered. "If I could choose?" Her eyes opened wide. She had a brief vision of the bare beach at Bradwell with the woods of Mersea Island framing the far side of the Blackwater River, and a stab of homesickness went through her like a physical pain. She could smell the salty grass along the sea wall and feel the warm, spongy mud of the saltings squeezing up under her bare toes. She thought of Toby, nimble on the deck of *My Alice*, and the dream cottage where the fire burned to welcome him, the ridiculous notion she had had when she left Bradwell. What fancies to reveal to Selina!

"Nothing much," she said softly. She thought of Selina's brother too, but there was nowhere he fitted in. He was the most ridiculous fancy of them all.

"But you wouldn't *choose* to be a housemaid?" Selina persisted.

"No, miss. But I wouldn't choose anything you would think was much. I'm happy now Toby's better."

"He means a great deal to you, doesn't he?"

"Of course."

"No, not of course at all," Selina said surprisingly. "I haven't given a thought to my brother all these weeks, and yet he's in danger as much as anybody, I suppose."

In spite of herself, Emily felt herself blushing at this reference to Adam. She said tartly, "The danger's of his own making."

"Well, yes. But even if it wasn't, I do not care as much as

I should what becomes of him. Not like my mother cares. Hardly as much as you care, I think."

She looked at Emily directly, without either censure or amusement in her last remark. Emily felt a wild indignation flare up inside her at the advantage Selina was taking of her in this unwelcome conversation, and said nothing. To her immense relief, Toby chose this opportune moment to open his eyes and utter a bored groan. Selina's expression changed, and she said, "The doctor says Toby can try his leg out in a day or two. I think he will soon be walking again."

In spite of Emily's first reluctance, she soon found that she was becoming more of a companion to Selina than a mere maid. As the weeks went by and Toby painfully learned to walk again and Selina saw her job coming to an end, it seemed that Selina was more and more loath to go back to her place in the drawing room. She made excuses to keep Emily in the guest room. As Toby recovered, his natural spirits broke down Emily's stiffness before Selina, and by the time he could walk unaided the sick room had become a place from where—Mrs. Briggs could hardly believe the evidence of her ears—laughter echoed out across the landings.

"If Miss Selina wants you as a personal maid, I shall speak to Mrs. Seymour about employing another girl for the house," Mrs. Briggs said severely to Emily. "The sooner your brother leaves this house, the sooner we'll see some work done."

"I'm sorry, m'm. I'm sure he'll be going very soon now."

"Just remember your place. Until I hear to the contrary, you're the housemaid here, not companion to Miss Selina."

"Yes, m'm."

Selina laughed at Emily's report of Mrs. Brigg's displeasure. But when Toby said he was ready to go back to work, Selina's amusement died.

"Oh, Toby, not yet!"

"Well, as soon as I have some clothes to put on—"

"I burned them."

"I haven't any more, miss!"

"Good. Then you'll have to stay. Or go to work in your nightshirt." Selina laughed. But then she said, sadly, "Emily, you'd better go and find some of Adam's. You know what there is in the closet better than I do."

"Yes, miss."

The door of Adam's room had been locked since he went away, and Emily had not been in it since she had tidied it after the search. She fetched the key from Mrs. Briggs, and went in reluctantly. She did not want to be reminded of Adam. In view of the fact that she hated him, she thought of him far too much as it was. And when she remembered him it was not as the Southend shark or the man who had injured her brother, but as a man who had moved his horse off the path to make way for her and who had called her the nicest maid his mother had ever had. Selina had been right about her caring. Emily despised herself. She opened the closet door and looked miserably at the well-pressed, unaired linen and the black coats on their hangers. The coats had the shape of Adam, broad across the shoulders and narrow in the midriff. From the satin gloss on the dinner jacket to the faded dullness of a riding coat, their limp neglect (a moth fluttered out past her face) saddened her. The whole room was gloomy, its back to the sun, its air still and stale.

A sudden tap on the glass of the long windows startled

her. She turned around and saw a man standing on the balcony outside. For a moment she stared, scarcely able to believe her own eyes. Then she heard the familiar voice through the glass doors, "Emily!"

She went to the window and shot back the bolts, trembling and stupid.

"Mr. Seymour! Sir, you—oh! Is it safe for you?"

The shock was so great she could scarcely form her words. It was as if the clothes she had been standing moping over had come to life and stepped out of the closet; the faded riding coat, faded almost to the color of the dust that covered it, the seamed and scarred boots with the spurs on them that had hung on the gas bracket. Emily could not believe it was Adam standing before her.

"What a welcome, my Emily! Is it so terrible to see me again?"

He did not look desperate or hunted, but perfectly cheerful. He was smiling at her in his old equal way, rubbing the sweat off his dusty forehead. He no longer had his curling side whiskers, and looked younger in consequence. He was paler too, as if he had been missing the sea winds.

"Oh, sir, it's such a surprise!" Emily whispered. She couldn't trust herself to say any more.

Adam flung himself into a leather chair.

"Pull my boots off, Emily. I've ridden all the way from London today. You should have seen Gregory's face when I rode in and handed him the mare . . . and what luck to find you here when I came in! Better than my mother." He eased the heels of his boots and Emily obediently pulled. "Don't tell her I'm home, if you can help it. Not for half an hour. Fetch me some tea and something to eat first, and a bottle of brandy. Unless they left me any. . . ."

He looked behind his bookcase. "No. Trust them to take a souvenir. Ask Mrs. Briggs for a bottle and bring it up quickly. Then I want to talk to you."

"Yes, sir."

Emily went downstairs to the kitchen. Mrs. Briggs was just lifting a tray of glass and cutlery off the table to lay the dinner in the dining room.

"A bottle of brandy for Mr. Adam in his room," Emily said.

It was the first and the last time she ever saw Mrs. Briggs responsible for breakages.

Adam ate and drank ravenously. Emily was commanded to stay, and between mouthfuls he questioned her as to what had happened since he had left.

"How is your brother?"

The abruptness of the inquiry roused Emily.

"He is recovering, but no thanks to you, sir" she said angrily.

"You should be thankful I didn't kill him," Adam said, unruffled. "When I left you, I wasn't sure. But later I read in the newspapers that he was hurt, but safe. Else, believe me, dear Emily, I should never have dared to come back and look you in the face."

"He very nearly died," Emily hated Adam's callousness, and even the "dear Emily" would not sweeten her. "It was your own sister that nursed him and very likely saved his life. He is here yet, in the room upstairs."

This information visibly surprised Adam. He stopped with his fork in midair and said, "Selina? You mean he was brought here?"

"Your mother told me to bring him here. And she ordered the doctor herself, and Selina to nurse him."

"And he's here now?"

Emily nodded.

"Good God."

Emily saw Adam's expression change. He reached for his brandy glass and drank slowly, as if he had forgotten in that moment that she was there. His thoughts were as clear to her as if he had spoken them aloud. Without waiting for further orders, Emily turned and left the room, slamming the door with a vigor that Mrs. Briggs heard two floors below.

A Dead Beat to Calais

"Yes, I dare say he asked very kindly after your health, but what was the real reason for his visit? Just tell me that—if you dare!"

Emily glared at Toby, who sat on the side of the bed looking so innocent and honest and unlike Adam that she could have wept.

"Why, what's up with you, Emmy? It's only natural he'd come and see me, I'd have thought."

"Oh, it's natural enough. But can't you see how his mind will be working? He used you once, and he needs you far more badly now. Not just to save his ship, but to save himself. What has he come back here for? He dare not leave the house, he cannot stay here. He wants to get to France, I swear it. And what has happened? He comes here and finds you at hand, more convenient than he ever could have dreamed. He will ask you to take him, if he hasn't done so already. I'm sure of it."

"Why are you so cross then? It's a simple enough task, if he wants it."

Emily's eyebrows shot up. "And what if you're caught? They won't let you off so lightly again."

"It's not very likely. They'd be a busy crew if they stopped to search every smack around these shores."

Toby had grown up. There was no defensiveness in his attitude as he looked at Emily, not even any great desire to placate her. In fact Emily had the feeling that he thought she was being foolish. Her anger fizzled away miserably. Perhaps she was.

"I know he's a wanted man, but I like Mr. Seymour," Toby said.

"Yes," Emily more than knew how Toby felt.

"If he wants anything, he'd better ask soon, because I told Miss Selina I shall be going tomorrow. You might be wrong, Emmy. How do you know what he plans to do?"

"I might be wrong," she agreed. She dreaded Toby leaving, now she had become so accustomed to having him under the same roof. "Are you sure you're fit enough to go?"

"I walked around the garden without any trouble this morning. I shall feel weak for a bit, I suppose, but I needn't start fishing right away. I shall be taking advantage if I stay here any longer."

Later that day, before dinner, Adam went to see Toby again. He stayed with him until the gong went, then returned again after dinner. He had been home two days, and the household, after the first shock, was reconciled to his presence and even anxious to protect him. Mrs. Noakes had sworn to God she wouldn't breathe a word about his arrival outside the house, and Gregory had already taken the mare by night to a distant grazing where her presence would cause no curiosity. Mrs. Seymour, Emily noticed, treated Adam with far more warmth than before, as if, acknowledging at last his shortcomings, she was able to accept him as he was rather than scorn him for falling short of her standards. When Emily had finished the washing-up and prepared all the bedrooms for the night, she went up to Toby's room to say good night. Adam had gone but Selina was there. Emily hesitated at the door.

"It's all right. Come in," Selina said. "I only came up to collect my sewing. Toby doesn't need a nurse any longer. He's leaving in the morning."

Toby was standing in the window, looking out into the

darkness. In Adam's clothes, so pale and tidy, he looked an uncommon smacksman.

"I shall see you again," Selina said to him. "You will have to report back to say if you delivered Adam safely."

"Oh!" said Emily. "So it's arranged?"

"Yes," said Toby gravely. "Don't say anything about it. It is settled. We are sailing tomorrow night."

"You're mad," said Emily. "You're mad to do it! I—"

"Emily, be quiet. I know perfectly well what I'm doing." Toby looked at her angrily and with an authority she had never seen before. She stopped in mid-sentence, and felt the rage and indignation coursing through her blood-stream like a fever. Selina looked at her pityingly.

"Come, Emily, leave him. Let them go, then it will all be finished and we can forget about them."

She took Emily by the arm and led her out on to the landing and shut the door.

"Go to bed," Selina said.

Emily went upstairs. Her feelings were so strong that she scarcely saw the familiar moonlit outlines of her small room. She was conscious only of the blinking revolutions of the lightship out in the estuary, the monotonous beckoning that had so strong an attraction for the only two people in the world she cared about.

"I will go too," she thought blindly. "I can't beat mats all day and not know what has happened to them. The fools! Why do they think it is so easy? Why do they make such trouble? Why can't we have peace and nothing to trouble us? I am so tired of worrying."

She felt she had done more than her share of worrying in the narrow refuge under the eaves, suffered far more excitement than she either desired or deserved since she

came to Southend. Would they let her come, she wondered?
She did not care about what Mrs. Briggs would say, or
even how Mrs. Seymour would react. Even if she lost her
job, she could not stay behind.

In the morning she caught Toby in the garden as he was
leaving. Gregory was driving him back to Leigh in the gig;
he had seen Mrs. Seymour, made an embarrassed farewell
of Selina, and now looked with some impatience at Emily
as she called after him. He was conscious of a great longing
for his old familiar world of men and boats and suddenly
felt he had had more than enough of emotional women.

"What's the matter?"

"Toby, can I come with you tonight?"

"Now who's being mad?" he looked at her, amused. "I
don't care if you come or not. What'll old Mrs. Seymour
say?"

"Oh, I won't ask her. She won't know till I'm away."

"Please yourself. I'm picking Mr. Seymour up at midnight, off the beach west of the pier. If you're there you
can come."

"Yes, I will."

In the cold light of day Emily knew she was being mad,
just as Toby thought. She watched him limp away through
the gate into the stables. She no longer felt afraid, but excited with an unreasonable, splendid, childish, old-fashioned
excitement, as if it were a party she was going to. She did
not think of the darkness and the mean, short action of
the estuary sea churning her stomach; she could smell the
autumn sharpness of the wind and she thought of *My Alice*
flying under kindly clouds and herself unfettered: Mrs.
Briggs, Mrs. Noakes, dust and polish and black-lead grates

swept into limbo, Adam delivered into freedom and Toby happy where he belonged, at the helm of a boat. She flung out her arms and took a great skip up the path.

"Eh, and what's up wi' you this morning, dearie? Got a flea in your drawers?" Mrs. Noakes was coming up the path behind her, laden with shopping bags. "Take me vegetables now. I'm fair panting."

Emily, startled into composure, took the shopping. "I was just saying good-bye to Toby. Gregory's taking him to Leigh."

"He's a nice young man, your brother. I reckon Miss Selina will be missing him. Eh—up, open the .door."

Mrs. Briggs gave Emily a sharp look as she went in. "Where've you been, miss? Mr. Adam's rung for his coffee. In bed, I might add." Her tone was withering. "Buck up with it now, then fetch the dishes from the morning room. Right hotel we are and no mistake, all this coming and going."

Adam, Emily suspected, preferred to take his early-morning coffee in his room where his mother would not see how lavishly it was topped up with brandy. He was not in bed, but wandering about in a plum-colored velvet dressing gown.

"Your coffee, sir." Emily put the tray down on top of his desk.

"Ah, good." He fetched his brandy from the bookcase and set the bottle on the tray. "Don't go for a moment, Emily. I want to talk to you. I have a confession to make, and I shall make it in good time on this occasion. Do you know what it is? Have you seen your brother since last night?"

"You mean that he's taking you to France tonight?"

"Oh, then I've nothing to confess then. You know."
Adam looked rather relieved.

"Aren't you angry?" he added.

"No. Not now. He says I can come too," Emily said.
Adam, in the act of pouring out his coffee, nearly dropped
the coffee pot. "The devil he does!" He stared at her
sharply, obviously not quite sure how to take this piece of
news, but Emily was full of her new-found excitement,
and would have defied him to stop her had he tried.

"You don't know how ill Toby has been," she said passionately. "Today is the first day he has been away from
this house since you left home! He will land you in France
all right, but what about his coming home on his own? Suppose the weather is bad? He has no strength at all—it's
impossible. At least I can help and do as he tells me." And
in her brain she could feel the bounding excitement. She
wanted to go! If Toby had been the fittest man in England, it would have made no difference to this unaccounta-
ble longing to put herself aboard *My Alice* and see the old
gaff swinging up the mast and feel the estuary breathing
under the black hull. Now that she knew she was going,
the reasons and the excuses were nothing. Even Adam
imprisoned could not feel as bound and stifled as she felt
all at once in the tall narrow house with the summer fading
and the sky above the mews as pale and clear as the sheen
on a pearl. She looked at Adam with her head up, eyes
positively glittering, and he laughed.

"Who am I to dare to stop you?" he said. "Your company
will make my escape a positive pleasure."

He took a sip of his drink and said suddenly, "I shall
need that opal necklace. Have you still got it?"

"Yes, sir."

It was still in the pocket of her dress where she kept it for fear Mrs. Briggs might find it, and she took a certain amount of pleasure in dropping it disdainfully on the desk. Adam smiled, and put it away in a drawer. But Emily was not concerned any longer with the significance of the opals, and was only conscious of this burning impatience inside her, this complete unconcern for the everyday routine in which she was supposed to be engaged. She never heard what Mrs. Noakes was saying, was surprised but indifferent when Mrs. Briggs rated her. She noticed that Mrs. Seymour and Selina were arguing again, and that Selina was crying before dinner, but it had no significance. It meant nothing. She laid the table, took up hot water, and laid out Adam's evening clothes.

When she served at table she felt as if she was acting in some ridiculous play. The smooth machinery of the sacred dinner hour had turned them all into civilized puppets: herself concerned only with the vegetable dishes and the serving spoons, Selina politely thanking her, while her eyes were still red and mutiny was bursting under her well-corseted silk bodice; Adam being the man of the house as if carving the mutton was his only concern in life, and Mrs. Seymour talking about the latest antic of Mr. Disraeli as if it was the only thing they could all be possibly be interested in. Emily handed the caper sauce and noticed that Adam had given himself an enormous helping, even while talking intelligently about Mr. Disraeli. It made her wonder what poor Toby had managed to glean during the day; she remembered the greasy sprats in the frying pan and the dank cuddy where Adam would take his next meal and she wanted to nudge him and say, "That's right. Eat up. You'll be needing it," but she only picked up his napkin which he had dropped and retreated with the remains of the mutton leg. Back in the kitchen she helped herself as generously as Adam, and Mrs. Briggs said acidly, "Fancy putting on weight, do you? You'll dream after all that." Emily knew she wouldn't get the chance, but said nothing.

"Not that you've been doing anything else all day," Mrs. Briggs added.

It was only when she got up to her room at ten o'clock that Emily began to feel she was coming alive. She changed out of her black maid's uniform and put on the old frayed skirt she had left Bradwell in and her own blouse and woolen jacket. The wind was in the southwest, fair and light, and the night was comfortingly dark, the lights of passing ships sharp as carriage lamps. Already Emily felt she belonged to the outside world.

She heard the bedroom doors slam and the bolts go home in the hall, and Mrs. Briggs snapping her closet door to in the room next door. Then there was silence until, presently, Mrs. Briggs's snores came softly and rhythmically like the purring of a cat. Emily waited for an hour, then she tied a scarf around her head, picked up her shawl, and crept silently downstairs. Adam opened his door at her soft knock and they confronted each other silently.

"Is it time to go?" Emily whispered.

"Yes, thank God. We'll go out by the balcony."

She went in. Adam was wearing fisherman's clothes with a familiarity that suggested they were far from strange to him. Emily had never seen them before and supposed that he kept them hidden away somewhere, possibly in the stable. Certainly she had never seen them in the closet. He snuffed the solitary candle on his desk, took Emily by the arm, and steered her over to the long windows.

"This is the worst part of the expedition," he whispered. "I shall feel happy when we are aboard. Are you sure you want to come?"

"Yes, sir. Quite sure."

They went on tiptoe down the iron steps. The tangled rose bushes stirred in the breeze and Adam lifted his face to feel the direction.

"As fair as if I'd ordered it," he said. Presently they were in the street and walking past the mews toward the front of the terrace. Adam held Emily's arm and she could sense the tautness of his grip. Their way lay along the top of the cliff to the end of the road and then down through the scrub and trees to the beach, and the road looked open and unfriendly, splashed here and there by a light shining from an uncurtained window.

Adam said, "It's a long time since I've felt happy outside without the mare between my knees." Emily could imagine his unease; she felt it herself now, yet it must have been with him ever since he started smuggling. The cold fear in the stomach, the thudding in the bloodstream: it sickened her, yet Adam seemed to thrive on it. He had never complained. They slipped and slithered down the sandy cliff, Emily as nimble as Adam in spite of her long skirts, and her fear changed to exhilaration again. Why should she worry for him, or even for Toby? Leaping and sliding down the crumbling sand, the escape was a game, like the Sunday she had spent long ago with Toby and Dick. She tripped and gasped, landing with a scrunch on the shingle. Adam said, "Hush!" sharply and she checked herself.

"Can you see the smack?" he whispered. "I can't—not yet. It's a hell of a dark night."

The tide was high, the water at their feet, ebbing out of the wheelmarks left by a bathing machine. Whoever, Emily

thought irrelevantly, bathed in October? The water was smooth and looked like black silver, slicking out with an impatient crusting of foam about the pier legs. The idea of swimming did not appeal to Emily at all; it was unnatural.

"What's that?"

Adam was staring out across the water. "How are your night eyes?" he asked her. "Can you see a sail out there?"

It was impossible to tell. Emily felt the nervousness coming back as they stood listening and staring. The night was very quiet. Some waders were whooping and quavering along the water line, and the shingle moved on the ebb with a soft whispering at their feet. A shell clicked and a crab rustled the sand, and far out on the Kent shore a tug wailed. The wail made Emily's scalp prickle uncomfortably. The estuary was wide and cold and black as pitch, and

the freedom she had wanted seemed suddenly a bleak desire.

"Listen! That's an anchor going overboard," Adam said suddenly.

Emily heard nothing, but presently she heard the rasp of a sail running down its forestay, and she saw the vague shape of a smack lying off. There were no lights, only a darker shape in the darkness. Shortly there was a soft splash of oars, and they were hurrying over the shingle toward the grounding rowing boat.

"Well done! Is everything all right?" Adam sounded as excited as a schoolboy. Toby nodded in the darkness, holding the boat steady.

"Yes. No one saw me leave that I know of. And I got stores on. Will you row, sir? I—"

He left his sentence unfinished and Emily looked at him

sharply, recognizing the exhaustion in his voice. She was already seated in the stern and Adam was shoving off. Toby climbed into the stern beside her as the boat floated, and Adam took the oars for the long plug out athwart the tide.

"Are you all right?" Emily whispered to Toby.

"Yes, of course. Only tired. I couldn't make out with a loaded dinghy against this tide. But don't fuss, for God's sake."

His asperity betrayed his weakness. Emily let his shoulder droop against her own, but said nothing more. Adam was perfectly capable of making his own passage to France and Toby could rest once they were aboard. He had got the smack to Adam and Emily could sense his satisfaction, even in his exhaustion.

They went aboard silently. Adam went straight to the anchor warp and started hauling it home, and Emily coiled it down neatly over the fathoms that lay unused. Toby had laid out the minimum for safety, and the anchor was soon barely holding the smack.

"Is the mainsail ready to go up?" Adam asked Emily, as if it were quite in order that she should be one of the crew. "I don't think Toby used it to run down, but we shall need it to clear the end of the pier."

Emily made sure it was unlashed, and Toby came forward and put the halyards in Adam's hands. Adam sweated up the heavy gaff, Toby ran up the staysail, and as Emily went aft to take the tiller she felt the smack take up on her anchor and ride off, eager as a loosed horse. Adam got the anchor inboard, cursing at its unmuffled clanks.

"Emmy, sheet in!" Toby hissed at her, "else we'll be under the pier end!" and he took the tiller off her, spilling the wind a fraction so that the weight on the mainsheet was eased and she could cleat it down. It was the job he would have done himself normally, but he now stood with his knee to the tiller, a cautious eye on the red light that shone on the end of the pier ahead of them. The smack was sailing close-hauled straight out from the shore, but the strong tide was bearing them down rapidly on to the pier, so that their progress was crabwise. Emily's eyes were on the red light too, and she thought Toby had misjudged, that the smack was going to be wrecked before they had started, but she dared not say a word. The stifling uncertainty froze her as she crouched down by the bulwarks. Even Adam, having set the jib and brought the sheet back aft to make fast, was standing watching the light, biting one thumbnail thoughtfully.

"She'll do it," he said, half questioning.

"Aye," Toby said shortly. "You'll see she's no *Bird* though," he added. "She'll point up no closer."

The black water slipped past. Emily could smell the stink of the wooden pier timbers, dank and weedy, making great caverns just beyond the boom end. She could sense the ungoverned pull of the tide beneath them against which they had no power; they could use but not cheat it, and if Toby had put them in the way of the pier the tide would crush and hold them fast against the timbers without mercy. It was nothing uncommon for a boat to go through a pier.

But Toby knew the limits of his smack and was used to making fine judgments. *My Alice* cleared the red light

comfortably and Emily was ashamed of her fears. Adam
freed the mainsheet as the smack came around on her new
course down the estuary and Toby handed him the tiller.

"You know the estuary, sir?"

"Yes. Don't worry. I've sailed this stretch by night more
times than I can remember. I'll use the Overland passage. You get your rest in."

"The lead line is just inside the hatch. The wind's backing slightly. It might blow up later so call me if you want
me."

"I will."

The only light on the smack was a small oil lamp lashed
beside the compass, with an old piece of sailcloth handy to
hide it with if necessary. Adam brought out his watch—an
incongruous bit of elegance to come from the pocket of a
cutch-stained smock—and noted the time, set his course
for the revolving flash of the Nore lightship three miles
ahead, and then trimmed the sheets to his satisfaction.
Toby went below. Emily knew she should go below too,
but nothing would have moved her from her place on the
deck at that moment, when the freedom she had longed
for all these dusty weeks had become a living thing all
around her. The loose spangle of lights on the shore that
was Southend was already well astern and fading, and the
old smack moved into the darkness with the eagerness of
Adam's mare. The wind was cool, the sky cloudy, specked
with a dim star here and there. With Southend fading, it
seemed as if the routine conventions of everyday life had
gone too: that she should be alone, sitting in the darkness
with Adam, was not strange, for they were the crew of
My Alice, not Mr. Seymour and the maid. Emily loved
Adam then, with a rare uncritical joy.

"Did you come this way in the *Maplin Bird*?" she asked. "Did they catch the *Bird* near here?" She wanted desperately to know more about Adam now that time was so short, and she felt no restraint in asking questions.

"They caught the *Bird* up in the Havengore creek, while we were waiting for enough water to cross the Broomway. That's the road that runs from Wakering across the Maplins. You can only cross over it at high water, and while we were waiting for the flood a boatload of excise men rowed up from Paglesham. We couldn't sail, we could only jump for it, swim to the sea wall, and run. Luckily, we had unloaded the *Bird* the night before and they found nothing aboard. Better the ship than ourselves, poor little *Bird*!"

Adam was smiling. Emily could see his face faintly lit by the compass light and his black hair blowing in the breeze. He looked every inch a smuggler, not a Southend house builder or dutiful son and mutton carver. Emily laughed. He glanced at her, amused too, and said, "Why did you want to come?"

"Why?" Emily could not put it into words. To come was an instinct. "I—I—oh, I'd have thought of nothing else if I hadn't! Sometimes I forget what the outside world smells like."

"Poor little Emily. Once I used to feel like that, before I had the *Bird*. When I was a law-abiding lad, doing what my mother told me."

"How long ago was that?"

"How long? When I was twenty-one I came into my inheritance, and I had my yacht built, and when I started to sail I saw that there were more interesting ways of making money than building houses. I met some fishermen round at Burnham, and some bargemen working up the Thames

and I learned how these things were done. Some of them
would come with me; we used to work together. They've
none of them been caught, nor me either, thank God."

In the back of her mind Emily recalled Dick's voice and
the complete assurance in its tone, saying, "The big ones,
they always get caught, because they don't know when to
stop." Had Adam stopped in time, she wondered? The
doubt tweaked at her present joy, and she watched Adam
gravely. *My Alice* rustled along; the only sound was the
hurrying of her black stem through the water, the slap
and dance of the overtaken tide on her timbers. Beads of
phosphorescence flashed and vanished like fallen stars.
Emily was acutely conscious of her magical transition from
everyday life, yet, her eyes on Adam, she wanted the
moments to hurry on so that this dangerous, beautiful flight
would quickly bring them to a prosaic safe shore. Adam
could hide away. After that—but Emily could think no
further. On board *My Alice*, for a few hours, she had good
reason to be happy; there was no point in thinking of the
afterward.

"You should go and sleep," Adam said. "You must be
tired."

"No, I'm not, sir."

She could answer him back; she could laugh at him.
Emily's eyes were sparkling, and Adam looked at her and
laughed.

"You deserve better than dusting, my Emily," he said.

Emily did not want to think about what she deserved.
She knew what she wanted, but what was the use of that?
She put her head against the hatch and looked up at the
swollen mainsail, gently swaying, darker against the darkness. The motion of the boat was easy. Never, Emily

thought solemnly, had she been so happy as she was now. She felt she must fix it in her mind, this happiness, to remember later when everything was finished. She did not think it would last very long.

My Alice had passed the Nore lightship, which marked the passage into the Medway, and was now heading into a velvet darkness. The only light ahead was the occasional flicker of phosphorescence in the bow wave. Yet Emily knew that the estuary was full of shoals, iron-hard sands that dried out as the tide ebbed and that would knock the bottom out of a hastening boat if her navigation was at fault.

"I've set a course that will see me to the West Spile buoy. From there the course is southeast by east three-quarters east to the Gore which will see us through open water off the Foreland. You will realize, Emily, that from the nature of my profession I prefer to sail in the dark."

"Of course. But how do you know when you get to the Spile? By hitting it?"

"That's one way, of course. But not to be recommended."

"How then?"

"By the time. We passed the Nore at ten minutes past one. We should be close to the Spile at two, at the rate we're traveling now. If we don't see the buoy we can sound with the lead to make sure we're clearing the shoals, then, if the visibility holds, we can pick up a bearing from the Girdler."

"The Girdler?"

"It's a lightship up in the Prince's Channel."

Adam knew this darkness then, as she knew the dark corners of the tall terrace house. Yet to Emily, *My Alice* was lifting her black stem to an infinity of danger. All the

wrecks she had heard of, and the wreck she had seen so
vividly a few months before, came forcefully to mind;
ships that had, one minute, been living, moving, hurrying
vessels, and the next crumpled corpses of wood and warps
scattered on the tide.

Adam was laughing at her. "So worried? Would you
rather Toby were at the helm?"

"Oh, no!"

"The *Bird* came this way often enough. Twice with a
revenue cutter on her heels at that. It paid to know the
shoals then, because I could take short cuts in the *Bird* that
the big cutters daren't risk. I put one aground on the
Shingles once. She'd have kept safe in the Bullocks if she
hadn't been so carried away with the idea of getting her
hands on my cargo. It would have paid them handsomely
and they guessed as much. But by the time they were off
I was home and the *Bird* was empty."

"You've taken some dreadful risks," Emily said. "I'm
glad it's finished. What would happen if you were caught?"

"I should go to jail."

"For how long?"

"A good few years, I dare say. I'd rather drown."

"Why do you do it then?"

"Why? It happened that way, I suppose. At first it was
a bit of fun, a lark. But it was so easy, too, and there was
all that money, just for having a lark. I enjoyed it. And I
think I enjoyed it all the more when it began to get dangerous. The *Bird* was such a splendid ship. She never let me
down."

"You mustn't start again. Not now, in France."

"I have no boat. I have some friends though. Look, Emily,
is that a buoy? On the port bow."

Emily went forward to act as lookout. The buoy was large and evil-looking, the tide foaming around its squat hull. The buoys were there to mark dangers, but in the darkness they were dangers themselves. *My Alice* heeled away, leaving it well to port, and presently Emily was able to pick up the half-minute flash of the Girdler lightship some five or six miles to the northeast. The night was dark but clear, and Emily was comforted by the steady prick of light. It was a friend to them, a conspirator in this secret sail. By dawn Adam wanted to be clear of the Foreland and safely at sea. Emily watched for him, and took the tiller when he wanted to sound with the lead line and was pleased with the fast, easy motion of the old smack. Even if she wasn't the *Bird*, *My Alice* was no laggard. The wind had backed slightly and was on the beam and she was reaching with a fine marbled bow wave tumbling over into the darkness. The sky was paling gradually ahead of them, and the dawn lamps of Margate fluttered dully on the shore. Emily yawned suddenly, and shivered.

"You're tired," Adam said, looking at her closely. "Go and get some sleep."

It was true. Emily didn't even have the strength to protest. She was no longer frightened, or happy, or even unhappy, merely tired.

"We've done well. We'll be clear off the Foreland by daylight and the wind is freshening. If it backs no farther, we'll be off Calais before dark."

If Adam felt tired, he didn't look it. Emily realized that this was the first time she had seen him at work, his restlessness channeled. He was as wiry and hard as any smacksman. The drawing room in the Royal Terrace seemed never to have existed. It was dark below. A candle still guttered in its gimbaled holder, and by its light Emily saw Toby's face white against the dirty mattress. He was sound asleep and did not stir. Already, she thought momentarily, he was the old Toby again, his hair uncombed and curling with damp, his pallor overlaid by the grime of a day's work. She thought of Selina, and of the satin-quilted bed and embroidered pillows, then she was burying her face in the straw mattress on the other bunk. Comparisons were blurred with weariness. Damp and shivering, she slept heavily.

She was awakened some hours later by a crash that made her leap up in her bunk. Hitting her head hard on the deck beam above, she cried out. Water was spurting up between the floorboards, and the smack was wallowing horribly; a heavy sail flogged on deck with great cracks that vibrated down through the frames and the sheets rapped along the decks with a noise like thunder. Emily saw that she was alone in the cuddy. Fear and nausea rose up in her throat together. She jumped to her feet and flung herself blindly toward the square of daylight that was the open hatchway. Immediately aft of the hatch was the mast, and she put her head up in time to see Adam snatch the coiled halyards of the gaff off their cleats and let the mainsail down with a run. The boom thumped down on the deck, followed by the mass of extinguished sail.

"Whatever—?" Emily could see nothing but gray wave tops all around them; there was no land in sight.

"The mainsheet has parted," Adam said briefly.

Toby already had his knife out and was cutting out the weak part. "I'll have it spliced in a moment."

"It's all right, Emily," Adam said suddenly, looking down at her.

She lay her head against the hatch, feeling weak with the fear that had passed over her. Then, as the smack rolled and plunged her bowsprit into a heaving sea, the feeling of sickness came again, so strongly as to put everything else out of mind. She scrambled out of the hatchway and half-ran, half-fell, to the bulwarks. Clutching the rail, she felt the deck heaving beneath her knees, and her stomach heaving in company. The water, gray as death, rolled up over the covering board, soaking her skirt and her thighs. She thought for a moment she was going to lose her balance, but an arm caught and held her.

"My poor Emily!"

Even while she was being sick, the great joke warmed Emily: the feel of Adam's arms around her, the faintest pipe dream of them all, and all because she couldn't control her feeble stomach. She laughed when she straightened up; the realist in her was strong.

"I—I thought—"

"Did you think we were in trouble? It's not bad. Are you all right, sweetheart?"

"Yes, I'm sorry. I—"

"Why be sorry?"

"Are you ever sick?"

"Yes. Lots of times." He had taken out a beautifully white handkerchief (laundered by herself, Emily guessed) and was wiping the spray off her forehead and pushing back the wet hair.

"Poor Emily. I can't think why you wanted to come."

"Can't you?"

"Ah, yes, perhaps. I'm glad if—" He paused, and looked at her, seriously. "I'm glad," he said.

Beside them the staysail started to flog, its sheet snaking down the wet deck. Emily glanced back at Toby and saw him look up in surprise, to see where Adam had gone to. She saw his eyebrows go up, then he put out an arm and pulled the tiller over to fill the sail again. His expression made her laugh.

"All right now?" Adam said to her.

"Yes, quite all right." She got up and shook out her wet skirt. She was cold, and felt dazed and stiff. Toby had his head down over his work, and she saw his fingers pushing and weaving the opened strands of rope one into another. His face was very noncommittal. Adam went to the tiller, glancing at the compass.

"This wind's still backing," he said. "We'll not lay our course shortly."

"No," Toby said. "Pity it's not Ramsgate we're wanting instead of Calais. This'll be a southeaster before the day's out."

"Oh, God, not Ramsgate," Adam said. "They know my face too well there."

Toby grinned. "We'll put Emmy on the tiller. That'll fox 'em." He hooked his marline-spike back on his belt and rolled his splice in his palm. "There. That's done. We can have our mainsail up again." He paused, and then said. "A reef would suit her, this wind."

Emily took the tiller while the two men put in the reef, then Adam went to the halyards and hauled the sail up again. Toby sheeted it in hard, and glanced at the compass.

"She'll not point up any closer. Southeast it will have to be."

He took the tiller and Emily said, "Where are we?" There was nothing but a gray hummocky sea merging into a low gray sky all around them. Sour white tops were breaking on the waves and the smack was crashing through them with a corkscrew roll that made Emily fear for her stomach again.

"We left the North Goodwin lightship astern about half an hour ago. We decided not to go inside the sands, because it looks like blowing up. We'll see no land now until we get to France."

Adam had coiled down the halyards and made his way back aft. Like Toby, he had a faded woolen cap pulled down over his ears; his smock was dark with spray. He looked tired, and Emily was not surprised to hear Toby say. "You can get some sleep in now, sir. I'm all right here —she's easy on the helm with the reef in."

"Very well."

"There's some bread and cheese in the locker, and a couple of bottles of rum," he added.

"Good," Adam fetched a bottle of rum on deck and offered it to Toby. Emily watched them take a turn each, tipping the bottle to their lips, but shook her head when it was offered to her.

"It'll warm you up," Toby said.

"Make me sick, more like."

"You're a sailor now," Adam said. But she shook her head, and he put the cork back. "I'll turn in then. Call me if you see anything," he said to Toby.

"Yes, sir."

He went below again, and Emily sat on the hatch, watching the waves riding up astern and the great holes that they left under their crests. Sometimes the smack's stem would drop into one of these holes with a crash, then lift her dripping bowsprit to the next wave as if it were a game she was playing, tossing a fountain of water over her bulwarks as she went. Toby grimaced at her antics.

"She's all right?" Emily asked anxiously.

"This is nothing." Toby said, as if to make up for the face he had made. "It's a pity we've got to beat into it though. It'd be easier on the old girl if we were running."

"What time shall we be there?"

"By dusk if the wind doesn't head us any more."

Emily thought, "Another eight, nine hours. . . ." She felt that the present episode was quite apart from her real life, as if she were in a dream. She did not delude herself. Adam was far more concerned with getting himself to French soil than with any moments of sentiment in the middle of a sail change, but for eight hours, at least, she could take a part in his life. Had to, in fact, whether he wanted it or not. The three of them were bound within the narrow frame of the old smack until they made a landfall. She could build what fancies she might, and pretend to her heart's content, but in eight hours it would all be back to normal, with the grim prospect of the return home the only reality to face. She shook her head impatiently. Her hair, heavy and warm, was falling loose beneath the scarf.

"You ought to get some food inside you," Toby said.

"Ugh. I couldn't."

"Are you warm?"

"Not very. But I'm all right. Are you?"

"I feel a lot better for a good sleep. Yesterday I thought I'd drop before I made the shore in the rowing boat to pick you up. I got the rowing boat back, you notice. That was a bit of luck. It was pulled out up on the wall at Leigh. And the money Mr. Seymour gave me is still in the mattress. It's the first thing I looked for."

"You earned it dearly! I wonder Dick hadn't been looking for it," Emily said bitterly.

"Dick? He's my friend."

"Ho! You think so?" Emily gave a snort of derision. "He wasn't much concerned about the state you were in when the customs men had finished with you. In fact, I've wondered, sometimes, if he told them anything."

"About what?"

"About Mr. Seymour, of course. They were around mighty quick after they'd decided you weren't the person they were after. You didn't tell them, I'm sure. You couldn't have."

"No."

"Did Dick know anything about what you had planned to do that night?"

"No. He only saw Mr. Seymour's letter, and that said nothing, save to meet him. No name was signed."

"It would have been enough for Dick to make something of," Emily said. "He's sharp."

"It did say the writer was a friend of yours," Toby remembered. "Dick said it was someone coming to ask for your hand." He chuckled. "He wasn't so wide off the mark, perhaps. I thought you hated Mr. Seymour, but now—"

"Oh, don't be such a fool!" Emily was furious.

Toby laughed. His eyes were on the sails, and he shifted to pull the tiller over a fraction.

"Your Mr. Seymour will be lucky to make Calais if the wind stays the way it is," he said. "It's going to be a dead beat all the way." His amusement faded quickly, and Emily knew that he was worried. "If this were the *Maplin Bird* now. . . ." he murmured. "Oh, Emmy, what a little yacht!"

Emily had no desire to think of the *Maplin Bird*. The sea would be no more gracious, even to the yacht. The waves were getting steeper, and the low cloud had given way to streaky, hard-edged banks, greenish from a struggling sunlight. *My Alice* was crashing along. Emily had to brace herself against the hatch to stay put. Toby had his back to the tiller, the whole weight of his body holding it over.

"We'll have to get more sail off her if it keeps on like this," he said.

A small shiver shook Emily, which was not entirely due to the cold. She remembered the water spurting up between the floorboards below, and all she knew of *My Alice's* condition. She could feel periodically the vibration of the old timbers as the smack dropped heavily from the top of a wave into the following trough. It was as if the water she hit were flagstones. The sea was not magical as it had been earlier, in the darkness; no friendly light offered salvation. Only the gray horizon showed in a complete, unbroken circle, touching the gray sky, and not a sign of life showed on it: not a sail nor even a sea gull.

"The wind's increasing?"

"Aye. We could do with our storm jib already. It'll mean waking Mr. Seymour though, to change sail. We'll carry on a bit longer and see how it goes."

"Couldn't I do it?"

"Good God, no."

Holding the helm down was tiring Toby rapidly, in his convalescent state, and Emily was not sorry when *My Alice* shipped a big sea which brought Adam up out of the cuddy to see what was going on. A large dollop of water had landed in his bunk; his awakening, Emily guessed, had been far less gentle than her usual discreet knock.

"Shall we get another reef in?" he asked Toby.

Toby brought the smack up into the wind and handed the tiller to Emily. She stood braced on the slippery deck, trying to stop the shivering and trembling of her cold body, amazed that this pitching, awkward drill appeared to be a commonplace to the two men. *My Alice*, slack in the eye of the wind, rolled and slithered down the glass waves. Her stern lifted like the back of a played whale, hung, and lurched down. Her bowsprit bit the next wave and the mast rolled across the sky as if it wanted to lie down. Emily's stomach rolled with it and she was sick again, but there was no one to comfort her this time, for Adam was getting in the sodden jib. The stiff sail flogged with reports like gunshot. Adam shouted to Emily to let go the sheet. Her hands were as stiff and numb as the hairy rope itself, her fingers redder than ever mere scrubbing had made them. She saw Adam secure the sail, lashing it down as if it were a struggling prisoner to be overcome, then the storm jib went out on the traveler, a handkerchief of a sail, and there was a sheet to be secured with the stupid fingers. Under the smack's stern a gray wave came at her like the side of a mountain, a tongue of foam rolling off the top, but *My Alice* rode up and the water hissed under her naked rudder.

"Hang on, Emily, for God's sake. Here—" Toby picked up the coiled mainsail lashing, knotted it around her waist, and made the other end fast to a cleat. He had tied down the reefs and Adam was waiting by the halyards.

"All right, haul away!" Toby shouted.

As the mainsail went up once more, and the sheets were made fast, *My Alice* started to sail again. The motion was easier than before, but it was a wet, wild ride.

"It's a dead beat for Calais," Adam said in disgust. "But at least we'll make progress while the tide's under us."

"If we put her on the other tack now, you can go below again," Toby said.

"Very well."

Emily began to lose all sense of time. There was nothing to measure it by: no land spinning by, no sun to cast a thin shadow. Adam slept, one hand dangling in the water that leaped across the floorboards. Toby eased his aching leg at the tiller and kept his thoughts to himself. Once, in a

gleem of steely sunshine, a cliff showed on the horizon off
the starboard bow, and Toby knew that they were leaving
England. The thought gave him more foreboding than joy,
and his eyes kept going to the frayed parts on his sheets.
But when Emily looked at him, he whistled tunelessly into
the wind.

Harbor

Adam slept for three hours, then came back on deck to relieve Toby. Emily, cold and sick, went into the vacated bunk, and Toby went below with her to get something to eat and drink. A spell on the pump had reduced the level of water in the bilges and he was able to sit with his legs braced against the lee bunk without getting his boots wet. He was glad to sit down, and ate ravenously, while Emily lay shuddering, trying to will the warmth of Adam's body out of the mattress and into her own frozen limbs.

When Toby had gone she groaned and buried her head in her hands. The water clouted the straining boards beside her head and roared in her ears. The smack groaned with her, and the sheets rapped on the deck above with a noise like a whiplash. Emily could not control the shaking of her limbs; whether it was cold or fear she did not know, but the effort it took to stop it was more than she could summon. She did not know whether she slept, or dreamed, or whether the things she heard in her ears were reality, but it seemed that the sea grew wilder, and the smack complained more bitterly. The bilge water rose up again and sluiced violently against the bunk. She heard Toby shout, and Adam reply, then the racket of sheets and blocks as the smack went into the wind and the sails started to flog.

The smack was going about again, and Emily changed bunks as the cabin took on a new heel. The stink of the stale wet straw in the mattresses made her retch. The precious hours that she had visualized earlier had long ago lost their appeal, and seemed to be stretching on into infinity. Calais was the world's end and lost over the horizon. Emily slept.

When she next awoke, someone had relit the candles. She could see a pair of leather boots on the companionway, and what seemed to be an alarming amount of water shining below her.

"It's no good. We're not keeping pace with it." The voice was Toby's, weary and cross. He was braced in the hatchway; Emily could see the whiteness of his face in the thin light.

"I'll free her off," Adam shouted.

"What's the matter?" Emily asked.

"Oh, it's all up. She won't take this weather," Toby muttered. He sounded too weary to cover up to Emily, too despondent to care. His voice and his words sent a coldness through Emily sharper than anything she had yet experienced. He looked down at her and saw the horror in her face.

"Don't worry. She'll hold together. But she won't make Calais."

He disappeared back on deck, and Emily gathered her wits together and followed him. *My Alice* was pitching and wallowing. Emily saw breaking crests in the darkness and, for a moment, far away on the port quarter, a small rash of lights low on the horizon. She did not know how long she had slept, only that the gray daylight had given way to a leaden, starless dark. Adam was working on the pump and Toby was at the tiller, freeing off the mainsheet. The significance of what he was doing did not occur to Emily immediately.

"What are those lights?" she asked.

"The French coast," Toby said.

He had worn *My Alice* around in a circle and she was sailing with the wind behind her, almost on a jibing course. The lights were now behind them. The motion was easy. The water hissed past and under the old smack, swinging her with it in a series of spectacular swoops. She was no longer crashing her way into the weather, but running before it, her boom freed out as far as it would go.

Toby watched the rolling of the boom end and said, "We'll have the mainsail off her."

Even under the two tiny headsails the smack moved through the water like a train. Her eagerness to leave the foreign coast was treachery, to Emily's mind. She looked at Adam's face, but saw no expression, only the sweat running down as he worked steadily at the pump. Emily dared not say anything. She was appalled at the turn of events. When she looked at Toby she saw that he was physically at the end of his tether, his wrists and hands shaking like an old man's and his breath short and fast. The look on his face shocked her into life.

"Can't I take her now?" she said. "I can do it, can't I?"

"Yes. Just keep her stern to the seas."

Emily reached for the tiller and Toby slumped down against the hatch. Adam stopped pumping to go and fetch the rum bottle. After the two of them had finished it between them, Adam took Toby below and Emily was left

alone on the helm, desperately trying to anticipate the his
sing seas that came running at their heels. There was so
much to horrify, suddenly, that her mind could make no
sense of it all. The tiller jerked and yawed under her raw
fingers as if trying to shake her off. The headsails were
quivering, the sheets thrumming with this alarming power
of which she was suddenly the master. Her sickness had
given way to devastating hunger, which now, in the midst
of this confusion, clamored for attention with a ferocity
that amazed her.

Adam came back and started pumping again without a
word to Emily. She could only guess at his feelings. She
was appalled for him, yet he showed no sign of anger or
even impatience at the turn of events. He pumped till his
hands were raw, then reported that the water level was
receding below. Emily asked him for something to eat, and
he fetched her half a loaf and a knob of cheese which she
ate with the tiller imprisoned in the crook of her arm. Her
hair had come loose and she had to turn her head so that
it blew free of her face while she tore off great ravenous
mouthfuls. Adam seemed to live on spirits. His face was
gray with fatigue.

"Shall I do that for a bit?" Emily asked when she had
finished eating.

He shook his head. "We're holding it now she's running.
She should hold together till we make Ramsgate."

"Ramsgate! But you said . . . you—"

"I must chance it. It's not only me now, with the smack
in this shape. It's all of us. She'll have to be beached. She's
making water like a sieve."

"But you were so close to France," Emily said softly. "I
saw the lights."

"Yes, but we weren't getting any closer. The tide was taking us off. And the wind has never eased—not once. It wasn't meant to be, I suppose."

"What will you do?"

"How can I tell? What course are you on?"

"Due north."

For the first time since they had set off, Emily was working her passage. She knew they were in danger, not from anything the law might do—that would come later—but from the sea itself. The battering the old smack had taken had proved too much for her. She was taking water in at almost the same rate as the pump was discharging it. Adam's strength would not last forever. He worked rhythmically, counting, then rested for a period, and started again. When Emily offered to relieve him again he did not refuse, but Emily was dismayed to find that she was exhausted almost as soon as she had started. She felt as if her heart were coming out of her side. Adam soon pushed her gently back to the tiller, and Emily compromised by giving him her scarf to wind around his blistered hand.

"What time is it?" she asked.

"About three. We should be off Ramsgate by dawn."

No more was said. They were both fully occupied. Emily was watching for the Goodwin lights, and longing for the first hint of light in the eastern sky, not because she was in any hurry for what the dawn would bring, but because she wanted the comfort of daylight itself. When *My Alice* rode up on a big crest, she would look all around, willing a sign of life to appear out of the darkness, the faint flicker of a distant shore window or the beam of one of the lightships, but the only relief was the breaking of the wave tops into a hissing surf. Once, turning around to see what was coming up behind, she thought she saw a red light far off the starboard quarter, but it was so unexpected in that direction that she thought it must be her imagination. She said nothing, but looked again the next time the smack's stern rode up. There was nothing there.

"You can make northwest now," Adam said. "We should be seeing something of the lightship shortly."

A few stars were showing over the mast top. *My Alice* plowed on, dropping her narrow black stem into the caverns of the sea, shaking off the manes of water that flowed back along her decks. Adam was resting for longer, gingerly stretching his raw hands and yawning compulsively. Emily prayed for the light, and saw it almost at once, pricking the horizon ahead. There was a streak of dusky purple over the wave tops to the east as well, as if the elements had decided to please her at last. She felt a surge of relief. Adam, having inspected the hold by the light of the oil lamp, was pumping again, his breath rasping with weariness. Emily, turning briefly into the wind to clear the hair off her face, saw the red light behind them again.

"What's that?" she said.

"What?"

"A red light astern of us. Over there."

Adam sprung up and stared. "It's a ship," he said. "Her port navigation lamp. She seems to be on the same course as us."

He hesitated, biting his thumb anxiously. "God, if only we could afford *not* to go into Ramsgate! She'll see us against the dawn presently . . . I wonder what she is?"

He went back to the pump, but his eyes were on the pinprick of red way astern. For all her tiny sail area, *My*

*A*lice was making up to the lightship rapidly. Rapidly, too, the lighter gray of dawn was spreading into the sky; Emily could feel, somehow, an inevitability about the way the journey was working out. Now, at its end, Adam was caught in a sequence of events that he must handle as best he could. The daylight was already showing their mast against the cold shell of hidden sunlight over the Kentish coast. To the mysterious ship to seaward she was revealed there like a spider pinned on paper, all the filigree of shrouds and sheets against the sky, just when Adam would have had her snugly wrapped in storm darkness, limping into port. Faintly now Emily could see a white sail above the red light and the gleam of a jib. Adam jumped up suddenly and started unlashing the mainsail.

"Put her up into the wind!" he shouted at Emily. "We'll have the mainsail on her again."

My Alice raced for the lightship. Behind her the spreading light revealed the distant ship—even to Emily, a familiar shape.

"It looks like—" She hesitated, and looked at Adam.

"Give me the tiller," Adam said, "and go and get Toby."

At last Emily saw alarm in his eyes. She went forward and down the steps into the cuddy. The water was higher than it had ever been, sluicing backward and forward over the floor. Toby was heavily asleep, and she had to step down into the water and shake him before he would stir.

"What is it?"

"Mr. Seymour wants you. There's a ship behind us. It looks like a revenue cutter."

Toby sat up and groaned. The sight of the water washing up against the bunk shocked him into wakefulness more promptly than Emily's words. He followed her up on deck, staggering with the stiffness in his leg.

Adam said, "If she catches us—" he jerked his head toward the cutter—"before we get into harbor, everything's up. But if we can keep ahead of her, there's just a chance. Take the tiller and I'll go on pumping.

Toby, now fully awake, looked around to get his bearings. The lightship was close ahead of them, marking the northern end of the Goodwin Sands. It was close on low water; once around it, they would have a six-mile reach inshore to the harbor. The cutter was still well behind them, but she was a vessel built for speed alone. *My Alice* was full of water. Toby could feel her sluggishness as he stood at the tiller.

"What vessel is she? Do you know her?" he asked Adam.

"I think she's the *Vixen*, the same one I put aground on the Shingles a few months back. They've good reason to remember me."

"But they won't know you're on *My Alice*," Emily said.

Toby thought. "They've good reason to connect *My Alice* with Mr. Seymour," but he said nothing. It was not apparent yet that the cutter was taking any notice of them, although she was on an identical course. They would learn her intentions soon enough if she altered course around the lightship to follow them. The lightship was abeam now, plunging on its gloomy mooring, its three great lights blinding the dawn. It looked deserted, but Toby guessed they were being well marked. As soon as they were astern of her, he put the helm down and started hauling in the sheet.

"I don't think she'll go any faster if we take the reefs out," he said. "She'll just lie over and take in more water."

Adam shook his head. His eyes were on the cutter. She had no such reservations for, as they watched, they saw a reef in her mainsail shaken out.

"She is after us then," he said.

"Likely she was sent out to search, after they noticed *My Alice* missing at Leigh. They'd piece things together, they'd know where you'd want to go to," Toby said.

Emily stared at the two men. They stood there, calmly appraising the cutter, accepting its part in the seascape without any signs of despair or regret. To Emily, it was the most dread and terrifying sight she had ever seen, throwing up a bow wave like a steamship. A wild indignation seethed inside her; a burning rage at their miserable luck, but Toby was merely saying, "I'll take a turn on the pump," and Adam was unwinding the scarf on his hand, grimacing as it came off the raw skin. He took the tiller. He looked at Emily and even smiled.

"What's your money on, Emily? *My Alice* or the *Vixen*?"

"Oh!" Emily almost spat. What if the cutter didn't catch up with them, she was thinking? There would be a reception committee all ready and waiting; already, no doubt, licking their lips at the spectacle to be seen through the spyglasses on the end of the pierhead. Adam's luck was running out fast; he had five—four—miles of freedom, and he didn't look as if he cared.

Toby said, "This is where you want your little yacht."

"Yes. She beat the *Vixen* a few times. But in these conditions—" He shrugged. "Even she wouldn't have the heels of that devil."

"We've a good start on her," Toby said.

Emily had pictured this scene a dozen times: the daring Adam Seymour pursued by a revenue cutter, blithe at the helm as he confounded his enemies. Perhaps, she thought grimly, he had been blithe in the past. But now, beneath the restraint she knew he was exhausted and scared. He was sailing the smack for his life, easing *My Alice* through

the big seas, his eyes going continually from his sails to
the distant harbor, to the outlying buoys and, every few
minutes, to the cutter behind them. Where for Emily the
smack had bludgeoned her way through the big waves, it
was as if, for Adam, they slid out of the way. White lips of
foam spun away from the bows.

Emily stood beside Adam, looking astern at the cutter. She wanted to say something to him but there were no words to express what she felt. She knew it was the end for him, and she knew that he knew, and that the cutter was the very personification of all the fears that had governed his actions ever since she had known him. She kept looking at him to see if he would show any feelings: anger or remorse or even downright fright, but it was as if he had drawn apart. His face showed only concentration, not emotion. It looked unfamiliar, the black hair flattened by the rain across his forehead, the eyes dark-rimmed with exhaustion. He was as remote from her now as he had been when she had still lived in Bradwell; she was as far from his thoughts as a shell on the beach. There was no kinship in extremity. Emily felt as if the cutter had already taken him. It made her sick to see the vicious curl of the bow wave springing up from the flared stem as it altered course to round the lightship, the eager efficiency of the sail-trimming. Each glance showed her perceptibly closer, her raking bowsprit leveled at her quarry like a lance. The sight chilled Emily to the bone. Already, in anticipation of what was to come, she was trembling inside her soaked skirts; she seemed to have no breath. She could see the walls of Ramsgate harbor ahead of them and the waves breaking in a mass of white foam on the windward side. The harbor lights had gone out with the coming of daylight, but lights were still shining from the houses that looked out from the cliffs. Gray squalls were driving up on the wind, occasionally breaking in a crackle of fury across the tight sails, and obliterating the coastline to both north and south.

"We'll beat her in," Toby said.

Adam said nothing.

My Alice, as if smelling her berth like a homing horse, crashed toward the harbor. A sea broke inside her swilling guts with every roll, but her bows still lifted and the foam streamed off her rudder. Emily could see a knot of people at the end of the east pier, outside the watch house, and she could feel the spyglass on them. No doubt there were eyes on her white face and streaming hair. Adam was watching the pierheads, to place *My Alice* to a nicety at the grim stretch of broken water that ran between them, and Toby was watching the cutter, which was beginning to take off sail.

"What are you going to do?" he said to Adam.

"I don't know," Adam said.

"There's no one on the west pier, but all the coastguards of Kent on the other, by the look of it."

Emily saw Adam's eyes go from one to the other, and back to the tide race at the harbor mouth. Behind him the cutter was crashing along in a cloud of spray. Emily could see the men ready at the mast to bring the mainsail down, and one on the foredeck who was shouting something. The thread of his voice came on the wind, but made no sense. Someone on the pier was shouting too. The harbor wall was very close, with the waves beating on it in swoops of white spray, seething against the stones.

"As soon as we're in, I'll put her up into the wind and you can get the mainsail off her," Adam said suddenly to Toby.

Toby looked surprised. "Why not let go the sheets and run her on?" he said. "It's a soft landing."

"No, you can run her on under her headsails," Adam said.

Ramsgate harbor, opening to the southwest, was designed

for craft to run into in a southwesterly gale, and bring up aground at the end of it. The water shallowed rapidly once through the pierheads. Toby had expected to do the obvious thing, but Adam's voice was firm and he did not argue with him. *My Alice* ran in close under the western pier, bringing up sluggishly as the wind was cut off under the wall. On the opposite pier by the watch house, Emily saw "all the coastguards of Kent" excitedly running about in the gray drizzle. Adam suddenly took her arm.

"Take the tiller," he said. He put her hand on it, and pushed it over with his own hand on hers, so that *My Alice* came up into the wind. Emily, startled, saw Toby run to the mast and yank the halyards free. The boom came down with a crash on the deck and Emily was engulfed in the wet mass of the sail. Adam had left her and she didn't know what to do, but the smack was docile at last. She shook her hair back, and saw Toby reaching for the gaff jaws which seemed to have stuck halfway down the mast. He shouted at her, "Sail her now!" and saw that *My Alice* was drifting into a trio of moored smacks ahead. She heaved the tiller back hard and Toby got the boathook and fended off while the old smack eased herself around and gathered way once more with the wind in her headsails.

"Put her on the beach," Toby shouted. He had got the gaff down and was frantically lashing down the sail. As *My Alice* sailed clear, the big cutter dashed round the harbor wall and spun up into the wind, her mainsail crumpling like a burst flour bag. Emily saw faces staring down at them, and a rowing boat coming down from the deck almost before the ship had brought up.

Toby was back aft and standing by her side. The old smack seemed to creep across the harbor, slowing gradually as her keel caught the mud.

"We're in trouble too now, Emmy," Toby said quietly. "You know that?"

"Where's Adam?" Emily said wonderingly.

She had only just realized why Adam had wanted the mainsail brought down. She looked around in amazement. A pair of leather boots lay on the deck. Toby kicked them underneath the bundled sail, so that they were hidden.

"He went over the side?"

"Yes, while the sail hid him from the pier. It was a good idea. Nobody saw him go, but they'll guess quick enough what happened. It might give him a chance."

Emily turned around, staring at the glassy gray water. The harbor was crowded with fishing boats and dirty colliers, mostly moored up against the wall or lined between buoys. There were dozens of mooring lines Adam might be clinging to, dozens of tarry hulls to cling to while the hue and cry ran past him to the limping smack that was—at last— still and listing on the mud.

"Let the sheets fly. I'll get the sails in." Toby said.

Emily felt completely empty of any emotion. The last

shock numbed her. Some men in uniform were putting out from the beach, and astern the rowing boat from the cutter was creaming toward them, four oars in perfect symmetry. Toby, taking no notice, was pulling down the staysail and unshackling it. Emily had no thought in her head but Adam. When the rowing boat slipped alongside she went forward and stood by Toby. Men boarded *My Alice* from all angles and another contingent stood by on the shore. Toby dropped his sail and put his hand on Emily's shoulder.

The captain of the cutter's gig ordered his men to search the smack and came forward to speak to Toby. He was a big man, and he looked angry.

"Are you Toby Garland, the owner of this smack?" he asked sharply.

"Yes, sir."

"Where is the other member of your crew? There were three aboard when you entered harbor."

"I don't know, sir."

"Lying won't help you. Who's this girl?"

"My sister."

"Who was on board with you when you came in?" the captain said to Emily.

She shook her head. She was frightened, suddenly, with all the fear she had imagined in Adam. She had never imagined it for herself.

"Who was it? Adam Seymour?"

The captain came up very close to her and she could see taut fury in his face. She remembered suddenly that his was the cutter Adam had boasted of putting aground.

"Answer me!" he said. His hand came up without her even seeing it and hit her across the mouth with a practiced flick that made her scream. It was so unexpected that the shock was stronger than any pain. She stepped back abruptly, and would have fallen, but Toby's arm held her. He stepped in front of her and Emily thought for a moment he was going to return blow for blow.

"Of course it was Adam Seymour! Who else do you think it was? Why else were you chasing us?"

"Where is he now?"

"God knows where he is. He went overboard."

The rapid search of *My Alice* had produced Adam's leather boots and no more. The first mate reported to the captain, who ordered them back into the gig.

"Take Garland with you," he snapped. "We'll hold him on board until we've got Seymour."

The coastguard contingent had already retreated and was sprinting back along the harbor wall toward the west pier. The search and interview had taken barely two minutes. Emily watched almost without comprehension as Toby was shoved roughly aft to where the gig lay alongside and forced aboard. The men were back at their oars, the captain in the sternsheets and the mate casting off. Emily ran forward and grasped the painter that the mate was just pulling free.

"Take me with you!" she said fiercely. "I'm as much to blame as him. You must take me."

"We've no place for women aboard, miss," said the mate, looking acutely embarrassed.

"Emmy, don't be a fool. Go back to Mrs. Seymour." Toby said. Her distress was worse to him than anything that had yet happened, and she saw the expression on his face. She straightened up and threw the painter down to the relieved officer. She could not bear to see Toby's agony of mind.

"All right," she said to him. "I'll be all right."

"Get the smack up to the high-water mark if you can," he shouted as the gig drew away.

Emily nodded. She and the poor old smack were Toby's only cares, and he was leaving them both in dire trouble. He turned around to shout something else, but the mate checked him with a well-aimed sea boot to the diaphragm which silenced him abruptly. Emily stared after the departing boat, tears streaming down her cheeks. She saw Toby hustled aboard the cutter and the search party start work. They were eager as a pack of hounds. She almost expected them to start baying. The thought that she might be a witness to their success was more than she could bear, and she went below. The water level was almost up to the bunks, but the darkness was her comfort. She lay on one of the wet mattresses, buried her head in her arms, and wept.

Adam's Last Sail

Emily had never supposed she would sleep in the midst of such a turmoil, but in fact she lost consciousness as if she had been felled, and only awoke several hours later when footsteps sounded on the deck above. Confused, and with a headache so piercing that she scarcely felt able to focus her eyes, she went up on deck, thinking it might be Toby. But two strangers—smacksmen by the look of them—were warping *My Alice* up to the wall. It was high water, and drizzling with rain. A glance showed Emily the cutter lying tidily to her warps, but no sign of any search parties. In fact the harbor looked deserted.

"She'll dry out comfortably here, miss," one of the men said to her. She noticed his curious look, and realized for the first time that she must be presenting a strange spectacle with her wild hair and wet clothes.

"Have you seen my brother? Is he still on the cutter?" she asked helplessly.

The smacksmen seemed to know what had been going on, for they did not ask her who her brother was, but nodded solemnly.

"Aye, they took him off up to the police station," one of them said.

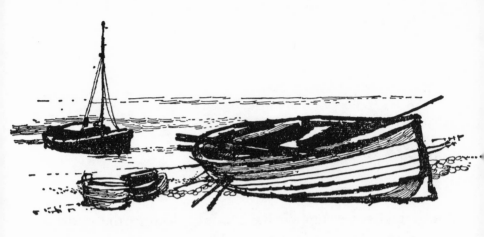

"And what about the other?"

"They've not come back, so I reckon they're still searching." The man looked round the old smack slowly. "This all you got?" he asked. "I mean, the only place to go? She's full of water, isn't she?"

"Yes," said Emily. A hot self-pity rose up suddenly inside her. The rain bounced on the shining decks.

"You'd better come along to my place and dry out," the man said. "My wife'll see you right."

"Is—is it far?"

"Just up over the road. She'll give you some dry clothes. You can likely go up and see your brother after."

For the first time Emily felt a gleam of hope. The thought of being dry and warm was too tempting to refuse. She was of no use to Adam any longer, and the smack was safe.

"Thank you," she said. "I would like to come."

The smacksman was a stocky, kindly man. As they went ashore and walked across the cobbles past the Customs House, he asked her, "Your brother was taking Seymour to France, they say?"

"Yes. But the smack was taking too much water and we had to run in here. Do you know Mr. Seymour then?"

"Oh, he's well known around her. Especially with the coastguards." He smiled.

"Do you think they'll catch him?"

"Aye, I reckon so."

"And what about my brother? What will they do with him?"

"If they catch Seymour they won't bother your brother much."

Emily asked no more. The man's words were a doubtful comfort. They crossed the road out of the harbor and climbed up a side street to the door of a terraced cottage. The man opened it and led Emily inside. A woman was cooking at a range and the warmth reached out to Emily, along with some delicious smells and sizzlings.

"Annie, this girl's had a rough passage. Perhaps you can find her some dry clothes and a bite to eat."

Annie's maternal instincts quickly got the better of her initial doubts, and soon Emily was sitting by the fire with a mug of hot milk in her hand, wearing Annie's own spare woolen skirt, caught together with several pins—for Annie was a plump woman—and a clean bodice and shawl. Her husband went out again, and Annie bustled around at her work, while the heat from the fire seeped into Emily like wine. Outside the rain beat on the windows. Emily wanted to enjoy her animal comfort and stared doggedly at the leaping flames, but all she could think of was Toby, shivering and ill, locked in some grim prison cell up the road, and Adam hunted by the coastguard pack along the rocks and cliffs. What an ending to their fine adventure! If only she had known what was in store when she had decided so

glibly to join them on the old smack. Her own comfort now
sharpened unbearably her feelings for Adam and Toby. She
wanted to leave the cottage and go up to the prison to see
if she could talk to Toby, but she dare not mention her
mission to Annie. She sat in torment, the tears scalding
down to salt her cup of milk, while Annie cheerfully
scrubbed the flags.

An hour later, Annie's husband came back.

"No news of your gallivanting friend yet," he said to
Emily. "Seems as if he might have got away."

Emily felt as if her heart had turned over in her chest at
the man's words. She nodded dumbly.

"We've got most of the water out of that smack of yours
now," he went on. "I doubt she'll take a lot now, nothing
that the pump won't clear anyway. I lit a fire in the stove
too. Let's have a bite to eat, and we'll go up to the—to see
if we can have a word with your brother after."

But the man at the police station had a face like granite.
He would not entertain the idea of his prisoner receiving
visitors. Emily went back to the harbor with her friend,
desolate. The gray sky had lifted to show a repentant afternoon sun, and its watery strugglings were gilding the harbor. The ships rolled in the swell, yards and masts moving
in uneasy arcs, warps tightening and freeing off, dipping
and lifting in the water with glinting drops rolling off the
chafed threads. There was a restless creaking and groaning
of strained fenders, and grinding of splintered wood. The
ebbing tide broke in disheartened waves under *My Alice*'s
keel and Emily looked down on her, quiet and orderly, her
sails stowed, her chimney smoking. Outside, the sea that
had nearly mastered her was tame again, merely sullen and
lumpish. *My Alice* looked positively domestic. Emily felt as
if this day had gone on forever.

"See, there are steps down for you. And there's a dry mattress aboard off my own smack. You can have it till your own dry out."

"You're very kind," Emily said.

They walked over to where the steps were let into the wall. The other smacksman who had been on board in the morning was leaning on a bollard and as they went past he said, "They've got him then."

"Who? Seymour?"

"Aye. He's on the cutter now."

Emily's eyes went to the ship. With the man's news she felt very calm and quiet, as if there was nothing to worry about any more. She expected to feel appalled, but she felt almost comforted. It was over.

"Oh," said the smacksman doubtfully. "It's finished then." He looked sideways at Emily. He saw her thin face very composed, her eyes very bright. "You—you're all right now then?"

"Yes, thank you."

"You call back for your clothes in the morning, and my wife will give you some breakfast."

"Thank you."

Emily climbed carefully down the ladder onto the deck of *My Alice*. The two men had walked away, and she was alone, back where she belonged on the old smack. She looked across to the cutter where she lifted and rolled on the swell across the harbor mouth, and she remembered Dick's prophecy, which had come true at last.

The weather cleared slowly. In three days it seemed as if summer had returned, the sky pale and clear and quite cloudless, and the sea smooth and shimmering like a spread of silk from the sands to the horizon. Gulls wheeled in the

sunlight above the cliffs. The ships left harbor and the topsails went up like opening flowers from the North Foreland
to the South. Emily watched them from the cliff top,
touched by their beauty. Never had October been so kind.
A warm breeze ruffled her hair; the air was sweet and
warm—"Kentish," Emily thought, aware of being a for-
eigner on this chalky cliff. It did not smell of mud and saltings and the sour tide of the estuary. It was the air of the
seashore proper, where chalk and sand introduced the land
to the sea. A clean beach lay below her.

She was entranced with everything she saw. She made a
great effort to be happy and enjoy it, because she was not
running up and down stairs with buckets of coal and sweep-
ing under the mats. She was her own master. She had the
twenty-five pounds of *My Alice*'s mattress in her bodice for
safe keeping and she could do as she pleased. For half an
hour up on the cliff top she could pretend, then when she
started walking back to the harbor she found herself hurrying to see if perhaps Toby was there, or the smacksman to
tell her some little snippet of news. She forgot all about her
independence. She ached with wanting to be in prison with
Toby and Adam, in the care of the granite-faced man. She
hated the granite-faced man, who would not let her in, nor
even take a message nor bring one out. He would not even
tell her if they were going to let Toby free or what his
sentence was likely to be if they didn't. Emily could do
nothing until she knew what was going to happen to Toby.

She went back to the harbor slowly, trailing out her time.
She had cleaned out and tidied the smack as best she could,
and the hours since had passed slowly. She was in an awkward situation, a woman alone on a boat in such a public
place, and preferred to stay hidden below when on board.

Curious people came to stare, and point her out to their friends, for the excitement of the chase was not quickly forgotten. This notoriety worried her; she would shut down the hatch and sit in the darkness rather than expose herself to their gossip. Once she knew what was going to happen to Toby, she could make plans, go back to Mrs. Seymour perhaps, if he had to stay in prison for long, but until she knew she could only wait around.

But when she got back to the harbor she saw that there was someone aboard *My Alice*. She stared, gasped, picked up her skirts, and ran.

"Toby!"

She scarcely touched the ladder but jumped, and fell in a heap in his arms, so that he was almost knocked flying. He was laughing. Emily could hardly believe the evidence of her eyes.

"What are you doing here? Are you free? Have they let you out?" She grasped his arms as if she expected him to vanish bodily before he had a chance to answer.

"Oh, Emmy, yes! Stop worrying. They've decided they don't want me any more. I didn't even get a fine. I think it was Mr. Seymour's doing, getting me off like that. And of course, they are so pleased to have him they weren't much bothered with me once he came in."

Emily could not take her eyes off him.

"Are you all right? Did they treat you well?" He looked well enough, she had decided. There was color in his cheeks and—she noticed for the first time—a fine golden stubble around his chin. She flung her arms around him and kissed him passionately. He laughed.

"I've been up to the police station a dozen times, and they wouldn't tell me anything. I thought they were going to keep you for weeks."

"Poor Emily! Well, it's over now. Is the money still in the mattress?"

"It's here, in my bodice."

"That's fine. Then we've nothing to worry about for a bit. We'll get the old girl caulked and sailing again, then decide what we're going to do." He looked around the decks and then across the harbor. The cold sunlight was fading and the sharpness of frost was in the air. "Oh, Emmy, there's nothing worth being in prison for," he said suddenly.

Emily sobered quickly. "Let's go below and light the stove," she said. "There's some food in the lockers."

The cuddy by candlelight, the stove burning driftwood, was as homely as she could make it. The floorboards were dry and scrubbed. Emily put the kettle on, and sat looking at Toby. Her happiness was extinguished now. When things had come right for themselves, it made it worse for the one who remained in trouble.

"What about Adam?"

Toby spoke reluctantly. "They're taking him to Sandwich tomorrow. They don't keep prisoners here, it seems. Then if he gets a long sentence, I think he goes to Canterbury."

"Is—is he all right?"

"Well . . ." Toby scratched his head anxiously. "How can he be? It's serious for him. Not like me." He paused. "They have no love for him, you understand, those coastguards that caught him. It took them nearly all day and they were angry. They took it out on him naturally. And then, up at the station, they want him to tell them who he worked with. They know there's somebody at Shoebury, and at Paglesham too. But of course, he's not saying, and that makes it—well, worse for him. It's only natural."

Emily shivered. Toby looked at her, troubled. "It's no good thinking, Emmy, that he doesn't deserve it. We like him, but there's things he's done . . . well, there's another side to him. Otherwise he wouldn't be what he is."

"I know," Emily said in a small voice. How many times had she told herself the same thing? She had forced herself to remember the Southend shark for her own good. What did it matter that he got what was coming to him? She steeled herself not to weep at the thought like a witless fool.

"He gave me an opal necklace because the coastguards were searching the house. He got it off that wreck we went to. Do you remember that old sailor telling us about the

Southend shark?" Her voice shook in spite of herself. "Did you know he was the Southend shark?"

"Yes. I knew as soon as I saw the *Maplin Bird*. I recognized the boat, and then when it turned out to be his . . ." Toby shrugged. "That's what I mean, you see. But I would help him again if I could," he added.

The weather served to underline their failure. The next morning, when Toby got to work on *My Alice*, the same pale, radiant sunlight warmed the harbor. A northeasterly zephyr scarcely ruffled the water.

"My God, Emmy, if only it had been like this!" Toby said. "If only we could have known!"

Emily looked at the cloudless sky and felt as if she were wrapped in a cloud of her own. She felt more miserable now than when Toby had been in prison as well. Then her despair had been as much for herself as anyone else, but now it was a completely hopeless, witless, useless ache for something that was quite beyond her own comprehension. She was astonished at the ingratitude of her instincts. She had all that comprised her own content: Toby fit and happy, food and shelter and money, her own freedom, the very sky above which she had hankered for in the Terrace; yet she scarcely felt alive, let alone happy. Toby whistled away down in the shingle, hammering in oakum. Little boys scampered and laughed along the quay.

Toby called up suddenly. "Look, Emmy! Do you want to say good-bye?"

"What is it?"

"Look, up the quay."

Out toward the pier end a small sailing boat lay against some stone steps. A man was getting the sail up, sorting out the halyards at the bottom of the mast, and at the top of the steps three others were waiting for him. One of them was Adam.

"Why! What's he doing?" Emily stared up, white-faced.

"Going to Sandwich. A fair wind and tide—they'll get up there at high water."

The men seemed to be in good spirits. The one in the boat was being chaffed about something, and Adam made a remark that set them laughing. By the way he was standing Emily could see that he was manacled by the wrist to one of the men, yet there seemed to be no animosity. When the boat was ready, Adam went down the steps with his warder and settled himself on the thwart. One of the men took the tiller and sheeted in the mainsail, and the remaining man shoved the boat off from the steps. Sluggishly, still sheltered by the wall, she gathered way for the harbor mouth. Not once did Adam look in the direction of *My Alice*. Toby looked at Emily uncertainly.

"Shall we go and watch them from the pier end?"

She nodded. They climbed up on to the quay and walked swiftly around to the west pier. Emily could not trust herself to say a word. She looked down dumbly as the little boat sailed clear of the harbor mouth and, catching the wind, started to throw up a bow wave, her faded sail tightening against the sheet. Adam had turned and was looking over the bows across Pegwell Bay where their passage lay; in the winter sunshine both water and shore glittered. Far away where the South Foreland made the last bastion of land against a milk-blue sky, a schooner's topsails caught the sun, bound down Channel. Emily saw Adam's face. It was all cuts and bruises, the hair blowing back, the eyes as bleak as the stones on the shore. He turned back and said something to the man at his side. A discussion ensued among the three of them. Then, after some cautious maneuvering, the man at the helm changed places with Adam. Emily saw Adam's fingers close over the tiller. He looked up at his sails and freed off the mainsheet, and the little boat increased her speed through the water, streamers of foam lacing her wake. For a moment Emily thought that the move was a ruse, some last desperate cunning designed in some way to effect another escape. But then she saw from the way that the boat kept on her course, drawing steadily into the shining arc of the bay, that there was no ulterior motive. No magic was forthcoming. Adam merely wanted to sail. He never looked back. Toby and Emily watched the boat in silence until it was just a faint dot on the flood tide.

Then Toby said slowly, "That's as cruel a way to go to prison as ever I could think of."

The Key

Mrs. Briggs opened the back door and positively snorted.

"Oh, miss, and what do you want? If you think your job's still waiting for you—"

"We should like to speak to Mrs. Seymour, please," Emily said.

"I hope you've got an explanation for your behavior," Mrs. Briggs said, opening the door grudgingly. "Running off without so much as by-your-leave." The fact that she had run off with the master of the house was not stated, but was obviously the reason for the strange looks Mrs. Briggs was bestowing upon her. Avid curiosity was clearly overcoming moral indignation. Emily gave Toby a nudge and he stepped reluctantly into the kitchen. The interview was one he dreaded.

"Has Mrs. Seymour had any news of Mr. Adam?" Emily asked, before Mrs. Briggs could get her own question in.

"She told me he had been taken by the police. That's all," Mrs. Briggs said with a sniff. "I can't say as I was surprised. I'm sorry for Mrs. Seymour, more."

"Was she upset?"

"Not as you could see. That was a week or more ago now. We didn't think as we'd be seeing either of you

again." Another curious stare raked the two of them. Toby shifted his feet uneasily.

"If we could just see her, and explain what happened—that's all," he said. "Then we'll go."

He had been working hard for a week on *My Alice*, stopping up her leaks; his hands were stained with pitch and his clothes were spotted and crumpled. Emily was well aware that she looked no smarter, although perhaps she was more in command of the situation than she had been on her first interview with Mrs. Seymour. Mrs. Briggs gave them another dubious look and said, "I'll tell her you're here then."

They waited side by side in front of the fire. Mrs. Noakes was not in yet, for which Emily was grateful. Toby yawned. He had sailed *My Alice* across the night before and was more ready for bed than anything else. This was a duty visit. He had tried to prevail upon Emily to go on her own, but she had prevailed upon him even more strongly to accompany her. As far as he was concerned the episode was finished; he merely wanted to get on with his work.

"She says to go up," Mrs. Briggs announced when she returned.

Emily heard Toby give a little groan under his breath. She gave him a fierce nudge and led the way up to the morning room. Mrs. Seymour was sitting as usual by the fire finishing her breakfast. She was dressed in black and had a black lace cap on her head, and she looked at them without any expression in her face, neither of welcome nor distaste.

"Mrs. Briggs told me you had called," she said. There was no invitation in her voice. "You have something to tell me?"

"I came to explain why I went away," Emily replied. She had forgotten how stern the old woman's eyes could be. She could feel all her brave answers melting away at the sight of the formidable figure across the coffeepot. She opened her mouth, stammered two syllables, then found herself gulping for breath. To her surprise, Toby said quite casually, "Mr. Seymour asked me to take him to France, and Emily came with us. If things had gone as planned, she would have helped me sail the smack home."

Mrs. Seymour's eyes went from Emily to Toby.

"He asked you?"

"Yes, ma'am."

"It was a job? He paid you?"

"Well, he would have, ma'am, if he'd had the chance, I dare say."

"Tell me what happened."

Toby did so. Mrs. Seymour nodded when the bleak tale was told, and looked at Toby thoughtfully. The hardness had gone out of her eyes and she looked merely sad. She sighed.

"I'm not sorry," she said. "It is an end to my worries, and no more than he deserved, although it is a terrible thing to have to say. I had a note from him this morning." She picked up a sheet of rough paper that lay beside her plate. "He tells me he has been sentenced to serve five years in St. Augustine's Jail at Canterbury. Nothing else." She put the paper down. "Five years is a long time to a young man. I only hope it will be long enough for him to come to his senses."

Although her voice was scornful, almost harsh, she was close to tears. Emily heard the news with an incredulous dismay that put every other thought out of her head. It was almost a physical blow, bringing with it a mental picture of the little boat reaching into the glittering sunshine. Five years! A convulsive shiver went through her. Mrs. Seymour was still talking but Emily hardly took in her words.

"I would like you to stay, Emily, for the time being. There will be some rearrangements here shortly. Miss Selina is going away, and Mr. Adam has already gone, but I will let you know my decisions later. I'm very grateful to you both for what you did for Mr. Adam."

They retreated in silence, and Emily saw Toby to the front door.

"Did for Mr. Adam," she said bitterly. "Did for him! Five years!"

Toby looked at her solemnly. "Don't think of it like that, Emily. He took a chance and he lost. We weren't to know. It's easy afterward to be sorry."

He went out and paused uncertainly. "Don't think about him, Emily. It'll pass." He sounded very fatherly.

She shook her head, too choked to speak. He went away and she went upstairs to her old room. When she passed Selina's bedroom door she heard her singing; the sound was so unusual that she hesitated, almost startled, and Mrs. Seymour's words came back to her: "Miss Selina is going away." But the momentary curiosity soon passed. For Selina to be singing heightened her own desolation. And this fresh self-pity maddened her.

"You fool!" she thought. "What if Mrs. Seymour had turned you out? You'd have had good cause to be miserable then! And what difference does it make whether Adam is in Canterbury or Calais? You'd never see him either way."

She despised herself for her wretched feelings, but could not shake herself out of them. The plain fact that she was desolate for Adam's sake was least consolation of all. She shook out her tangled hair and took vengeance on herself by attacking it with a fine comb.

"Romantic fool! Lovesick servant girl! Discontented pig! Thank God it wasn't Toby moldering away in jail as well, or yourself too, come to that! We could just as easily all be at the bottom of the sea and drowned the way it was, and you wouldn't even be here to be miserable!" But Adam had said he would rather drown than go to prison. "The imbecile! To drown is forever. Doesn't he know? It's just one of his lies, to talk like that." And she remembered his face again, looking across the bay. And earlier how he had put his arms around her when she had been sick. It made her laugh then, but it did nothing to cheer her up now. Her steeliness quite deserted her, and she thought of him in his Canterbury prison, in rough prison clothes with his hair cropped short and the cathedral bells pealing in the sunshine, and she started to cry with uncontrolled gulps and sobs, the tears raining down her blouse.

"Why, Emily, whatever is the matter?"

She had not heard Selina's knock, and was horrified to see her standing in the doorway. She groped desperately for her handkerchief, unable to say a word.

"What is it? What's wrong? Is Toby all right?" Selina's blue eyes were shocked. She closed the door swiftly and crossed over to the retreating Emily. "Is Toby all right?"

Emily nodded.

"But what is it then? You haven't got to leave, have you? Mother never said. . . . Why are you crying? It's not like you."

Emily mopped her face and made a great effort to stop crying. Never, not even when her parents had died, had she felt such a wildness inside her. There was nothing of awe and bewilderment now as then, only this wild and sudden passion which had seized her. She backed up against the window and tried to take a steady breath.

"It's—all right."

Comprehension flashed in Selina's eyes. "It's Adam?" She looked at Emily almost with relief. "That's it, isn't it? Oh, Emily, don't!"

But Emily had quenched the outburst and looked numbly at Selina. She knew what Selina was going to say.

"Emily, he's not worth it."

"It doesn't make any difference," Emily said. "It doesn't make any difference at all, what he is or what he isn't." God only knew, she had tried hard enough to make it matter. She straightened up and shook back her hair. "I'm all right now. I didn't mean to—to be like that. It's finished now."

She remembered Selina singing and her own moment's curiosity. Selina looked very excited and pretty, in a crimson dress with a swaggy bustle caught up at the back and a creamy lace cravat pinned with a pearl brooch.

Emily said, "I've seen Mrs. Seymour and she asked me to stay. But she said you were going away." She wanted to stop Selina looking at her in a pitying way, and the prompt was successful.

"Yes, it's true!" Selina said. "Mother says I can go to Queen's College in London. I can hardly believe it! I am going to my aunt in Bloomsbury tomorrow, and then to the college to see the principal. Oh, Emily, I am so happy! And you are so sad." Her face fell suddenly. Emily had never known her so warm and human, and wished she could respond instead of standing like a petrified block, swallowing down the tears.

"What—what made Mrs. Seymour change her mind?" she asked.

"When the news came that Adam was caught, she was very—well, very upset. She said—she said we had both failed her, and she no longer cared what we did. So I asked her if I could go to London and she said yes. I mean, she could hardly refuse, having said that." Selina's eyes sparkled. "I know you will think me heartless to behave like that, and heartless to feel that Adam, for once, has done me a good turn, but I cannot help it. It means too much. But I shall work so hard. She will be proud of me in the end, I swear she will."

Emily supposed she might, too. But she would never be proud of Adam.

"I'm very glad for you, miss," she said.

It was very quiet when Selina had departed. Even Mrs. Briggs and Mrs. Noakes said they missed her untidy ways. The torpor of the house suited Emily, who felt she had no feelings left at all. She had been shocked by the grief she had shown to Selina, and spent all her time making out a case against Adam, enumerating the reasons why she should despise him. She was able to convince herself without any difficulty that the indications that he cared nothing for her far outnumbered any to the contrary. Even his last gesture, that of putting his hand over hers, had been primarily to push the tiller over. Just as his holding her in his arms had been to stop her from going overboard. "Really," Emily said to herself, "it is very funny. It should make me laugh." But it didn't. Nor did the fact that he had not said good-bye, or thank you, or even looked at *My Alice* when he had gone away. With her old logic Emily exorcised the unnerving sentimentality that had possessed her. Adam was no better and no worse than he had ever been. Responsibility for her misery lay at her own door, for letting her feelings take charge. Nobody had ever made out that Adam was worth loving, least of all himself.

Selina was successfully enrolled as a student at Queen's College, and Mrs. Noakes left, as there was no longer enough cooking to keep her occupied. Emily looked covertly at Mrs. Briggs as they ate their breakfast, and was aware of the great, sad silence that had settled on the house during the last few weeks. Even Mrs. Briggs was not so brisk any more; there was much less work and far more time. In fact, the empty time, as far as Emily was concerned, stretched into infinity. She could see herself sitting in Mrs. Briggs's place thirty years hence, with her red hands and stringy wrists. . . . Never satisfied, she said to herself. She sniffed, and sprinkled coarse sugar on her porridge.

"You ought to get that morning-room carpet up, Emily, and give it a good going over on the line."

"Yes, Mrs. Briggs."

"And scrub underneath while it's out, and lay clean news-paper. I'll leave you some out."

"Yes, m'm."

"And fetch Mrs. Seymour's dishes when you've finished your porridge. I'll start the soup."

When Emily went up Mrs. Seymour was standing looking out the window. It was a gray day with an easterly wind blowing up the estuary. Some bawleys were beating out to the Kentish side, knocking up a white foam under their bowsprits. Emily began to stack the china on the tray.

"Is your brother quite recovered from his injury these days, Emily?" Mrs. Seymour said suddenly.

"Yes, thank you, ma'am," Emily was surprised.

"I have been thinking, Emily, that he lost a great deal of working time, thanks to Mr. Adam, and has never been properly rewarded."

"Mr. Adam paid him twenty-five pounds, ma'am, when he tried to move the *Maplin Bird*. And then you saw that he was properly cared for afterward. That was worth more than any money."

"Is he still living in that dirty cottage you described to me."

"Yes, ma'am, as far as I know."

Mrs. Seymour said no more until Emily was ready to leave the room, then she said, "Emily, I told you a little while ago that I was making different arrangements in the household. You realize, now that Mr. Adam and Miss Selina have gone, there is no longer much work here?"

Emily put the tray down slowly. Never satisfied, she repeated to herself coldly. Now there would be good reason to cry, if she no longer had a job. She looked at Mrs. Seymour blankly.

Mrs. Seymour said, "Mrs. Briggs is perfectly capable of waiting on me, and doing the laundry and the cooking. And with most of the rooms shut up, the cleaning can scarcely take all day."

"You mean you no longer want me, ma'am?" Emily said.

"I cannot find employment for you all day, Emily. But I have an arrangement in mind that might suit you." She came across to the table where Emily stood and smiled suddenly.

"Don't look so scared, child. I'm not going to turn you out on the street."

Emily waited, dubious.

"I have come to the conclusion that it would be better if you lived out, and came up here to work for just a part of the day, from six in the morning till two o'clock, perhaps. One of my cottages down by The Ship has come empty, and I think it would suit you very well. You could have your brother to live with you, which would be more suitable than his living in that hovel at Leigh. When he is established you would pay me rent of course, but for the time being, I should not ask for anything."

She looked at Emily closely, as if nervous that Emily

was going to dissent. She saw a tumult of expression pass over her face.

"Oh, ma'am, you—I—" Emily could not get the words out. It was as if Mrs. Seymour had put a match to a fuse; Emily's griefs, hopes, fears, and self-reproaches exploded into an overwhelming moment of joy. There were no words to express it. It passed, of course; it was immediately diluted with doubts and caution, but it was not wholly quenched. The promise of security and freedom gave her a warmth that she had not known since her parents died. In fact, the feeling was so strange that it was some moments before she realized that she was still Emily, standing with a tray-ful of dirty crockery, tongue-tied like an idot, while Mrs. Seymour waited for her reply.

"Oh, yes, ma'am, thank you. I—we should like—it would suit us very well. Thank you, ma'am."

"When you have finished your work tell Mrs. Briggs to let you off so that you may go visit your brother. Later I will give you the key, and you can look at the cottage. If any repairs need doing, I will see to them."

"Yes, ma'am, thank you."

To her great embarrassment Mrs. Seymour then said, "You are a very good girl, Emily. I want you to be happy. You have not looked very happy lately."

"Yes—er, no, ma'am." Emily cautiously picked up her tray.

"Your troubles have come to you early in life, Emily. It is far better than their coming late, like mine." She spoke softly, and Emily scarcely heard her. In fact, she did not think she was intended to. Mrs. Seymour was looking out of the window again, and Emily backed to the door.

"Is that all, ma'am?"

"Yes."

Oh, it is enough! Emily thought. The day passed in a dream. She visited the cottage with Toby, and they stood at the bare window and looked across the muddy road and the beach to where *My Alice* rode to her anchor on the edge of the curdled estuary. Their voices echoed off the damp walls.

"I can still fish with Dick and the others, but unload here instead of at Leigh," Toby said. "It's as handy as a place could be."

"And at two o'clock I am free!" Emily said softly. She could light the fire for Toby coming home, as she had always dreamed about.

"I suppose the old lady has done it because of what we tried to do for Mr. Seymour. It doesn't make sense otherwise. No rent!"

"For landing him in Canterbury," Emily said. She meant it bitterly, as she had said it before, but it wasn't, in fact, as bitter to her any more. The hurt feelings (for that was all it was, she had told herself) had shelled over like a raw hull with barnacles. There were still gaps, but the wildness she had revealed to Selina had gone.

Toby said slowly, "Mr. Seymour and Miss Selina have both, in a sense, got what they deserved. Perhaps that is what has happened to us too. We have tried, both of us, for what it's worth."

"Conceit!" Emily said.

Toby grinned. They went out carefully and locked the door, and Emily put the key in her pocket. They stood for a moment, Toby looking out toward the smack and the unrelenting yellow water which he now thought of as home, and Emily conscious of the weight of the key against her thigh. Emily could think of nothing to say which would convey her strange sense of freedom, and yet of belonging; oddly, Selina came to mind again. Toby was right, perhaps. She smiled. She did not think of Adam.

They parted, and went their separate ways.

ANN A. Flowers, Patricia Lord, and Betsy Groban edited the introductory material in this book, which was phototypeset on a Mergenthaler 606-CRT typesetter in Primer and Primer Italic typefaces by Trade Composition of Springfield, MA. This book was printed and bound by Braun-Brumfield, Inc. of Ann Arbor, Michigan.

Gregg Press
Children's Literature Series
Ann A. Flowers and
Patricia Lord, *Editors*

The Minnow Leads to Treasure by A. Philippa Pearce. New Introduction by Ethel Heins.

The Maplin Bird by K. M. Peyton. New Introduction by Karen M. Klockner.

Ounce, Dice, Trice by Alastair Reid. New Introduction by Elizabeth Johnson.

The Sea of Gold and Other Tales from Japan by Yoshiko Uchida. New Introduction by Marcia Brown.

Dear Enemy by Jean Webster. New Introduction by Ann A. Flowers.

Mistress Masham's Repose by T. H. White. New Introduction by Ann A. Flowers.